LEECH

JOHN C. FOSTER

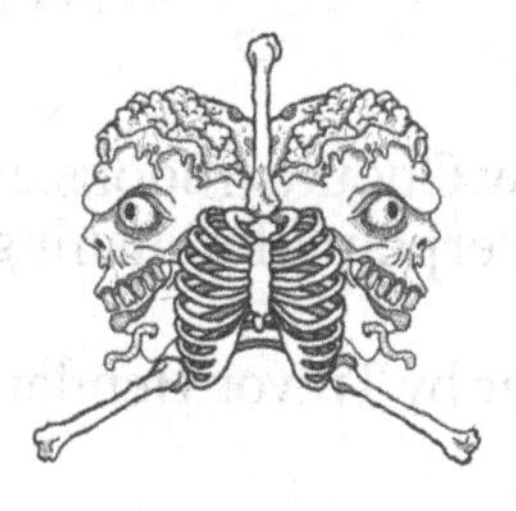

Ghoulish Books
an imprint of Perpetual Motion Machine Publishing
Cibolo, Texas

Leech

ISBN: 978-1-943720-70-5

www.GhoulishBooks.com
www.PerpetualPublishing.com

Cover by Trevor Henderson

ALSO BY JOHN C. FOSTER

Dead Men
Night Roads
Baby Powder and Other Terrifying Substances
Mister White
The Isle
Rooster

THE FIRST STORY

1.

LOW CLOUDS SCRAPED the tops of the Ozarks and Leech hoped it wouldn't rain. He remembered learning how to tell the difference between the Ouachitas and the Ozarks, what his granddad called the Hillbilly Hills. The Ouachitas were proper mountains with something in the way of peaks, whereas the Ozarks had been pressed flat, as if God put down a hand and leaned his weight on them.

The road narrowed and began to wind up the mountainside before Leech screeched to a stop, Bertha vibrating before the white and tan County Sheriff's car pulled across the road. He keyed off the ignition and listened to her engine tick in time with the buzz of insects, dabbing the hollow of his throat with a handkerchief and chewing on a minty toothpick. He studied the sides of the road and saw birds flitting among the coarse pines and bent oaks, the space beneath stuffed to bursting with rude shrubbery that would tear his linen suit to shreds. It was green with life and black with shadow and resisted the existence of the road mere feet away.

The deputy who eventually emerged was significant of belly if not height and his boar's bristle of hair revealed rolls of fat at the back of his neck. If the mullet was designed with a particular man in mind, it was this deputy. Unfortunately, he deigned not to wear one.

"What you smiling at, boy?" The deputy loomed at Leech's window, his gut threatening to come inside. Leech studied the belly before him, noting the strained buttons, the tiny black hairs curling through the diamond like separations of fabric where the shirt strained the hardest. He wished the man had worn an undershirt but realized it was awfully hot.

"You hear me, boy?" The deputy stepped back a pace so he could stare Leech down with his mirrored sunglasses, inflating Leech's smile by surrendering on the second damned move of the game. Leech pushed his Panama hat back and flipped open his billfold to flash a little sunlight at the deputy.

"Oh, well, yessir," the deputy said, that high school bully cop tone slinking away to be replaced by something unctuous. "I didn't realize—I thought there'd be more of you. Trucks, hazmat suits and all that."

The local law raked his gaze up and down Bertha, noting the mosquitoes in the Lincoln's grill and the dust around the wheel wells. "Aren't you a bit . . . underfunded?"

A flick of the tongue fixed the minty length of wood dead center between Leech's front teeth and he grinned around the wood. After an awkward paused the deputy said, "But don't you need—"

"Son, what did they tell you happened up in Durable?"

The fat man adjusted his gun belt, which caused a small temblor across his midsection and threatened the shirt buttons. "That little lab up there had a outbreak."

"*An* outbreak."

"Right," the deputy said, missing the language lesson.

Leech rested one pale sleeve on the windowsill and leaned out. "Do you think they'd really tell you the truth?"

"I—it's a cover story?"

"It's a cover story."

Leech was beginning to feel like a kid who pulled the legs off flies. He roused Bertha from her stupor, the big engine filling the air with an almost subsonic thrum.

"I'll just move my prowl car then."

"Thank you, deputy."

LEECH

Leech was grinning just a little bit as he drove past the County car and wound uphill, the light succumbing to shadow as he climbed. He disliked those beady-eyed types and while it was a flaw in his own character, found it hard not to tease them—

"The Battle of New Orleans" bugled from his pocket and he gave himself a mental kick for forgetting to call Karen. Bertha agreed to a stop and he set the emergency brake before pushing the door open with a screech of hinges to let in a little more air.

"Hey," he said, when the phone found his ear. A hot wind pushed the treetops alongside the road and caressed the beads of sweat on his brow. He sent a prayer of thanks to the inventor of linen suits.

"I'm so sorry, baby," Karen's voice pleaded across the miles. Leech knew she was and said as much.

"You drinking?" he asked, and she said not so much and he said that was good.

"You ain't going somewhere dangerous, are you?" she asked.

"Not to worry, honeybee, just some little hillbilly town where things have gone funny."

"Oh no, those inbred fellas will make you pregnant and I don't see you as the daddy type."

"I promise to use protection."

She giggled. "Got your gun?"

"No," he lied. "Not that kind of job."

"You got Bertha?"

"Yes," he truthed.

"Bertha's a good old gal and will take care of you."

"Always has."

"What are they callin' you this time?"

"Archibald Leech." He didn't tell her he'd chosen the name.

"Like Cary Grant?"

"Except with two Es."

"Terrible." She laughed and he touched the shiner beneath his left eye. It was a fair trade if he could keep hearing those sounds of joy.

The conversation went the way of such things and she was calmer at the end, promising to only drink a little bit more, which calmed him as well.

"Remember to take your pills," she said.

"They don't let me out unless I do," he said as if it was a joke and not a damned fact.

"My secret agent man." She sighed across the miles.

"Your secret agent man."

They said they loved each other and he hung up, putting away the phone and drawing his Luger to check the magazine. He bent low, the movement awkward because of the big steering wheel. His sensitive fingers grazed the twin-barreled derringer on his right ankle and touched the coil of a wire garrote wrapped around his left.

He sent a quick text message and the red light on the dashboard lighter blinked green, unlocking the small air-powered injector that had to be released from Control. If he tried to do it himself (he had) a heating coil fried the dose.

"Geronimo," he muttered and pressed the injector to his neck, grunting as it popped a load of Activator into his system. He didn't know what chemicals were in the Activator—some kind of formula more secret than the Colonel's—but it burned the Clozapine and Risperidone from his veins like a brush fire.

The sweat dried on his forehead as his normal brain chemistry kicked in. It usually took a minute so he tapped the radio alive and spun the dial through static to discover choices ranging from preaching to country music to preaching accompanied by country music. He pondered Bertha and Karen and thought himself a man gifted by the company of good women. Light flashed off the windshield and he spurred the big Lincoln into motion.

The scales were lifted from his eyes.

2.

Bertha obliged Leech by slowing when they drove around a bend and saw three people jumping up and down beside the road. In the middle was a hardscrabble woman in a shapeless housedress, displaying the squinty eyes common to these parts. Today, however, her peepers were as big as could be and her lipless mouth was stretched wide enough to show the gaps in her teeth. She leapt up and down, attention fixed on something overhead. Bouncing on either side of her were a boy and a girl in colorless hand-me-downs, neither more than ten. Fear ruled their faces.

"Afternoon, ma'am," Leech began when she laughed in his direction.

"Outta that car, son! Don't want to bang off the roof!" As if on cue, a bright red cardinal smacked onto the Lincoln's black hood.

"Why y'all jumpin' around?" Leech asked, pouring gravy over his words and ignoring the dead birds sprinkled over the asphalt.

"It's the rapture! We gone be raptured!" The woman jumped high enough that her children were jerked like fish on a line. "Jump, children! Jump on up to His Kingdom!"

Leech craned his neck out the window to study the gathering clouds overhead before taking a little video of the group with his phone. He panned beyond them and zoomed in on the colorful spatter of a robin. Beyond that was the broken form of a crow.

"Jump! Jump!"

Leech made the mistake of studying the little boy's face as his lips formed the words, HELP US.

"Try kickin' off those shoes," Leech called out. "Lord don't want dirty shoes in his kitchen."

The woman stopped bouncing in place as her face blanked, then warped into another grin. "Right, *right*!" She kicked off her shoes. "Get those shoes off," she screeched at her kids. Leech continued up the road until they were lost around the curve, pretending he couldn't hear the crunch of bird bones beneath his wheels.

He checked the mechanical clock on Bertha's dashboard and the green glow of the radium dials allowed that it was only 3:00pm, despite the deepening gloom. He thumbed his phone to text the video back to HQ (among his many sins was a proclivity to text and drive). When the photos didn't send he grimaced at the improbability. Bertha had a powerful wi-fi transmitter in her belly and dispensing messages was not usually a problem.

The tree line opened up to the right and he muttered, "Alright then," as he cruised past a shadowy graveyard ringed by a tilting iron fence. A small crowd of people were digging at the graves and shattering tombstones with swinging shovels.

One by one their heads turned his way, faces distorted by extremities of emotion.

Leech already knew that Durable was going crazy and didn't much care about their particular story, so he dropped his foot on the gas.

3.

Bertha opened her eyes with an audible snap and powerful halogen rays wrenched details of road and tree from the concealing darkness. It was 3:11pm and might as well have been midnight. He drove slowly, aware of scuttling in the underbrush, once slamming on the brakes when a passel of boys darted across the road, naked as jaybirds.

The stink of burning things rode heavily on the air. Pulses of pain clutched the back of his jaw. He filmed what he saw. The scampering children, a smoldering pile of furniture, deer bounding downhill, but was still unable to send the messages back home. Embracing the Boy Scouts' motto, he undid the snap on his shoulder holster. He wondered if Durable was actually a town or nothing more than hillbilly shacks scattered up the mountainside.

The ivory house with its long verandah was something of a surprise and he slowed, taking in the old man in the rocking chair who read beneath the amber glow of a hanging lantern.

"Ho Atticus," Leech said, stopping the car to step out and touch the brim of his hat.

"I'm no country lawyer, son." His lips curved in a smile and sent seams running across his dark face.

Leech grinned before waving a hand at the night. "Whole mountain's going crazy and you're sitting on your porch?"

"Spent a long time building this porch and I aim to enjoy it while I can."

"Things are that bad?" Leech cocked his ear at the patter of rain.

"Can't you feel it?"

"Fillings in my teeth hurt."

"My titanium hip is vibrating like a guitar string." The old timer leaned forward in his rocker and lifted a perspiring glass of sweet tea from beside the chair. "I'd invite you to join me but you look like you're here for answers." He cocked a head. "That rain?"

Leech could see specks falling through Bertha's headlight beams and jumping beans bouncing off the hood. He swept his palm across the warm metal and grimaced at the smear of bugs.

"Dead bugs," Leech said.

"Well, that'll happen."

"So you can see it too?"

"What?" The old man arched an eyebrow in confusion.

Leech covered with a question. "Is there a bit of town to Durable?"

"What there is you'll find when the mountain gets flat and the road levels out. Less'n a quarter mile."

"Obliged." He glanced at the sinister press of clouds, lit from below by the town's glow up ahead. A trick of the light gave the roiling masses the appearance of glowing from within. Of teeming with shapes that defied recognition.

The rain of bugs continued to fall.

"Government man come to see what the other government men got up to?" the old man said.

"Something like that." Leech lifted his hat and raked his damp hair. "You know what they were doing up there?"

"The DARPA folks? Working on a camera, a new kind of camera that sees through to beyond."

Leech felt the first chill of contact as his mind engaged with the reality outside of his skull, like a submersible seeking to equalize pressure with abyssal depths.

He ditched his chitlin act. "How do you know?"

"'Cause I've seen it. Most of us have. Hell, they started beaming the picture to everyone in town." The old timer grinned around blocky dentures.

The *crack-crack-crack* of a high-powered rifle drifted downhill. Leech nodded at the sound. "After seeing the picture, everyone suffered a psychotic break?"

"I seem psychotic to you? Most people are in their homes, praying or fucking or crying, the things people do when the TV screen turns to snow."

"And the rest?"

The old timer fanned himself with his book. "Some people are just assholes."

A tumbling bat bounced off of Bertha's roof.

4.

Leech said, "Shit!" as light flooded the Lincoln and the grill of a pickup truck rushed at his window. The sound was enormous. Too vast for definition. His spirit was blown out of his body and the world tumbled.

5.

Tiny hands.

"No more pencils . . . "

Tiny teeth.

"No more books."

The wildly tattooed boys were too small to drag him all the way from Bertha's embrace. His legs still lingered inside her body while the car itself rested on her roof amidst the bushes.

"No more teacher's dirty looks!"

A kitchen knife punched into his shoulder, not deep but painful enough to rouse Leech from his stupor. He flailed an arm and the boy scampered back with his bloodied weapon raised like a trophy. Another boy lifted a rock over his head and hurled it at Leech. He grunted as it bounced off of his ribs but it focused him and he saw their bright, wild eyes. The splashes of blood playing the part of tattoos.

"You get deten—" A boy with a Louisville slugger stopped mid-word when the Luger materialized in Leech's fist.

They scattered, hooting and screeching like animals as he writhed free of Bertha and fought to stand upright against the pain of sprung ribs. He touched a finger to lips that had been mashed against his teeth before spitting out blood, knuckles whitening around the Luger's grip as he pushed through the undergrowth towards the sound of grinding gears, ignoring the thorns that ripped at linen and skin.

They were scrambling like a troop of baboons atop a pickup truck with smashed headlights when he stumbled onto the road. The engine roared and the truck lurched before stalling. The starter motor whined and Leech sighted down his arm, aiming just over the hood because the driver was short.

The windshield starred and the grinding starter motor stopped. An animal screech was flung from the truck's grill, which looked so much like teeth. He didn't know what the truck was trying to become and had little interest in finding out. A finger twitch sent a second bullet through the grill and into the guts of the vehicle.

Bodies tumbled and the wild boys scattered as he sent rounds hurtling after them. A twitch of his thumb released the spent magazine and he slapped a fresh one into the butt of his pistol.

The iron sight settled between bare shoulder blades before Leech caught himself and lowered his arm. What was he doing? This was not a moral question, he had no sympathy for the savage younglings who had snared him in their trap.

He was wasting ammunition. He was not in control.

He had to stay in control when he was Activated.

Leech touched his head and wondered if he had banged his skull harder than he thought. His fillings were vibrating enough to pop from his teeth and he spat out another mess of blood. He had his doubts about old Atticus' understanding of events in Durable. Something was at work on the people and seemed to be slipping tentacles into his own mind. He wondered what the invader found inside his noggin, if it found something to grasp onto or if it, in turn, found itself caught like a fly in a trap.

He pushed hair back from his head and brushed some bugs free, wishing he still had Bertha—or, failing that, his hat. "If wishes were horses," he muttered and wished he had a horse. Having none, he resigned himself to the heel-toe express and limped up the road.

He passed a brick school building spitting fire from its windows, the roof ablaze like a thatch of wild red hair. The misshapen lumps in the yard were likely corpses, but Leech ignored them in favor of a wooden sign welcoming him to town with the words A FRIENDLY PLACE.

The sign ticked as it rocked in a fresh breeze and a rain of water replaced the fall of chitin and wings. Leech tilted his head back and let the rain cool his face, staring at clouds crouched close overhead like children studying an anthill.

He stuck out his tongue to catch a few drops before walking on, reaching out to tap the sign with a finger in passing.

He was in Durable.

6.

Silent lightning danced below the billows of dark cumulus, presenting snapshots oversaturated with light so that the town appeared as a series of washed out black and white photos. A vision of the past.

He leaned against a light green pickup truck with the rounded hood common to the '54 Chevy and fought against vertigo. The pain in his fillings pulsed along with the electrical discharges in the sky. It was as if time had lost its way, which might explain the lack of sound effects accompanying the light show. When the thunder caught up to the present, he expected it would be a doozy.

The payphone was a welcome anachronism and he squelched through mud surrounding the general store to lift the receiver from the hook, straining to listen past the sound of rain drumming on the awning overhead.

At the hum of the dial tone he hung up and patted a pocket, irritated when he didn't hear the jingle of coins. If the DARPA facility didn't have a working line, he could hoof it back to the payphone and make his report, but he needed change.

He lifted a dripping shoe to step over a yellow bicycle resting in a puddle, smiling vaguely at the playing cards clipped to the wheels. He did that himself as a boy in . . . where was it? Savannah. He grew up in Savannah.

Mud splashed from his shoes as he mounted the peeling wooden steps and opened the door, a bell tinkling over his head. He clopped across the plank floor to a candy counter, hunting for Mounds Bars. He used to buy a Mounds and a Coke on the way home from school with his lunch money. The red and white package prompted a grin. He had so loved sweets as a boy . . . he dropped the candy bar to rub both hands against his face.

"Shit-shit-shit." He recognized the time slide, the time glide, the time ride. He needed his Clozapine. He needed—no, he was Activated for a reason. Durable. DARPA. A camera that sees through to beyond.

He moved past shelves of canned dry goods, glad that the lights had been left on. "Hello?" The beer cooler was empty and a pleasant drift of cold wafted from the still open door. He leaned inside to enjoy the icy air when movement at the edge of his vision—

It was only the store cat slinking towards the dark rectangle of an open door in back, presumably leading to storage.

Leech closed the glass door of the beer cooler with a swipe of his hand and fished a bottle of seltzer water from the next cooler, twisting off the top and chugging until he let loose a ferocious belch.

He stiffened at a muffled thump from the back room, eyes straining to pierce the darkness.

The cat must have knocked something over. That was all.

He armed moisture from his forehead and took a Coke before picking up his Mounds Bar from the floor and approaching the counter. He'd eat and drink his fill before picking up his bike . . .

They were seated behind the counter, faces blue with death, lips speckled with foam. Recent deaths then, the champagne and empty prescription bottle resting in between the man and woman suggested their method of escape.

"What the hell?"

Leech pressed the heels of his hands against his temples and rubbed vigorously. The counter cut into his belly as he leaned over and stabbed buttons on the cash register until it opened with a DING. He scooped out a fistful of change and ignored the bills. He needed to call headquarters and tell them . . . what? Please FedEx six hundred straight jackets to Durable, stat? That he'd shot a few kids re-enacting *Lord of the Flies*?

DARPA. He had to make contact with the facility before reporting. Smeared letters were written in the blue ink of a ballpoint pen on the back of his left hand. PILLS.

Did he write that?

"Screw it." He snatched something from a shelf and spun to the door—

A pale face thrust itself at him.

"Jesus!"

It was his own ugly mug reflected in the glass.

He pushed his way outside and stood beneath the awning to commit his sin. Whispery lightning continued to flash as he unwrapped the cellophane, resigned to whatever complaints Karen might share if she smelled the transgression on his breath.

The first drag off the Lucky Strike felt like he'd inhaled a crown of thorns. He coughed, smoke bursting from his mouth, eyes watering. The nicotine rush hit his system and he felt lightheaded before his lungs remembered their old friend. He walked with steadier steps out into the street, weird wisps of fog curling around his ankles.

Down the main drag, trudging past monochrome houses from another time. When he saw a stirring in the low mist, he dismissed it as another cat, perhaps the store cat following him in the hope of a meal. The chiaroscuro suggested motion where there was none. A corner-of-the-eye shifting that tied his nerves in knots. He was striding across the set of a Hammer film instead of Durable, Arkansas.

A shotgun roared nearby and he heard muffled wailing. Fleshy smudges hinted at faces behind windows, marking his passage. Eddies in the fog revealed a pale back and he stopped until his path was clear, unsure if he had seen a man or a dog.

When he passed between two churches facing each other across the street, he noted that the Seventh Day Adventists had won their war against the ill-prepared Methodists, who were scattered in wet lumps on the lawn below the smoldering remains of their wooden church. He caught the mouth-watering odor of a pig roast and knew that at least a few folks had died in the fire. The slaughter seemed to call for a gesture or words, so he said, "Fuck," and slogged onward

His cigarette was hanging like a limp dick by then and he dropped it into mist that had risen to his knees. The image of those wild boys crawling low beneath the fog came to him, knives clutched between their teeth like TV pirates. His gun found his hand and he passed it back and forth across his wake but saw nothing that warranted shooting.

Maybe the totality of his report should be, "It was schizophrenic, baby! There was never a town." They'd pack him off to a padded room and never tell Karen where he'd gone. He laughed at himself for thinking that where they kept him was anything better. The saltbox house he shared with Karen was no more than a gilded cage.

"I'm coming, honeybee," he promised and knew he would get home. He'd crawled out of the Pine Barrens when things went strange and staggered away from the Yukon when reality ripped loose. He was the secret weapon they unleashed when the fabric tore and alien mathematics leaked into the world. The agency nobody had heard of wielding him like a barely understood instrument.

Because he could see through the curtain.

He could see.

He could see.

It was enough to drive a man mad.

The crash was enormous and he jumped away from the sound, stumbling over the mist-shrouded curb to sit hard, banging his teeth together.

For one terrible moment he was fog blind, patting the wet ground in search of his pistol. Everything was grey and noises became muffled and strange. Slowed down, as if the sound waves stretched like toffee.

Skin met metal and he clutched the pistol, sitting up so that he was neck-deep in the treacherous vapor.

The fog rolled like a returning tide back towards a house across the street, having been pushed away when the entire front of the dwelling fell forward onto the lawn.

A woman was standing on the second floor in her nightgown. Though her mouth was stretched wide in shock, she never stopped filming with her phone as the grey mist swarmed in to cover the fallen façade of her home. It was as if she needed to dilute the moment to a digestible onscreen experience.

Something caught her attention and she pointed her device at Leech when he rose from the swirling grey. "Did you see that?"

Leech ran.

"Hey! Hey!" She shrieked after him.

The red disk of a STOP sign offered escape and he darted onto a street named for a tree, continuing until the violated house was lost to sight. He slowed and spit, breathing harder than he should.

A thin-lipped smile was ruined by the sound of singing. Many voices coming from a street hidden behind houses. Enthusiastically mournful, the kind of dirge the Adventists enjoyed hollering.

"Five bucks says they're at the DARPA facility," he said to no one as he broke into a jog, coughing up gunk from the cigarette. His steps splashed on the wet road as if he were wearing clown shoes instead of sleek Italian leather and he hoped the singers would keep making noise. A bright flash revealed a narrow turn between trees and he jogged beneath an arch of drooping branches as leaves fluttered down around him.

It was a government ugly building of poured concrete, surrounded by a chain link fence with signs reading KEEP OUT and PRIVATE PROPERTY. Powerful emergency lights blazed holes in the surrounding fog and the flat metal roof banged like a kettledrum under the downpour.

A few heads turned his way and the singing trailed off as the smack of his shoes slowed.

They were at the DARPA facility.

"Fuck."

7.

Leech froze.

As the Adventists turned, they winked out of existence before abruptly reappearing, gaping mouths aimed in his direction. If they had turned in unison he would have written it off as a trick of light and fog, but because they turned in ones and twos, he was able to dissect the marvel.

They were a two-dimensional phenomenon, so thin as to be non-existent when viewed from the side. Living, breathing cardboard cutouts clutching knives and gardening tools and in one woman's hand, a black stained rolling pin.

As loyal in its own way as was dear Bertha, the Luger cajoled his hand into sudden movement and set to barking. Hurtling lead punched holes in the leading fanatics and they wobbled as people do when receiving the Luger's gift.

"Hoooey . . . " Leech said as beams of light sprouted laser-like from their torsos, the incandescent rays powered by the glowing emergency lights of the facility behind them. Mouths opened and they spoke in rapid clicks before fluttering down to fold atop themselves like summer weight curtains sliding off the rod.

"Alright now."

His six remaining rounds put paid to the remaining phantoms and they fluttered off to wherever two-dimensional Adventists go.

That their tools bounced off the road and stayed behind put a dent in the theory that they were hallucinations, as did the dark stain that coated the site of slaughter. Raindrops speckled and spread the gore and he thought Karen might laugh at the gape-mouthed expression he wore.

LIGHT AND SOUND.

Leech was on his knees, hands clutching his ears as the noise of colliding worlds shook the very ground. He glanced up to see if the moon had fallen from the sky and got an eyeful of rain for his trouble. He had a sense that things were accelerating, the final act announced by Gabriel's trumpet.

The thunder was here.

8.

Leech was blinded by lights. His toes scraped over the ground as two men in white dragged him into the fenced perimeter of the DARPA facility. It occurred to him that they were ruining his shoes.

"Who are you?" asked one of his rescuers.

"Whaaa?"

The gate rolled shut behind them with a rattling crash.

THUNDER.

All three of them were on the ground, the men in white writhing like beetles as Leech pushed up to his hands and knees, working his jaw to clear his ears.

He grabbed a fistful of lab coat in each hand and pulled, struggling against a ground gone weirdly mushy, as if the earth was reconsidering the idea of being solid. He made out the dark oval of a woman's face behind a window in the door and screamed, "Let us in!"

9.

The brushed steel table was covered in computer printouts and a *Star Wars* calendar was thumb tacked to a wall. Red streamers danced in the airflow from a vent near the ceiling. Colored security monitors showed swirling grey as clouds and ground fog joined to form an impenetrable mist. Plaster dust sifted down from the ceiling with each boom of thunder. It was the kind of office that would benefit from a nudie calendar and a fridge full of beer. It was the kind of office that killed the world.

"You're it?" This was Goetz, the lady in charge.

"I'm it." Leech's billfold was in her hand. Sweat slid down his glass of iced tea and formed a ring on the table, a mirror image of the rainwater puddling beneath his chair.

"I thought there'd be more," Tweedle Dum said.

"Not that it matters," Tweedle Dee said.

"Why you?" Tweedle Dum asked.

"I'm special." Leech tapped a finger against his temple.

He wrote off the milk-white lab boys and focused on the round lady with the glare like a nail gun.

"Tell me about the camera," Leech said, tossing aside the stapled papers they gave him, drips of water flying from his linen sleeve. "You got X-ray vision, can see the color of my drawers? You peeking at those funny obelisks on Europa?"

"We thought—" Tweedle Dum began until Leech cracked a palm down on the table. Thunder shook the room.

"I don't care what you thought it would do. What *did* it do?" He aimed a finger at Goetz. "These boys irritate me, you talk."

Goetz stood and waved her male companions into silence. She stepped to a wall monitor and her fingers danced over the keyboard mounted below it.

"We were playing with light and gravity and thought we might be able to see through time. The plan was to film it and study what we saw."

Leech took a moment to let that one process. "Why?"

"Well, if we could see backwards, we could solve all manner of mysteries. If we could see forwards . . ."

Leech sipped his tea and took a moment to think. Ice cubes clinked. "But you saw something else."

"We saw something else." Goetz tapped the screen. "See this room?" It was a black cube with rubberized surfaces and some kind of machine in the middle, aiming what might be a cannon at a gleaming titanium sheet on one wall. It looked like a tank pulled up before a drive-in movie screen. A white-coated corpse was sprawled beside the machine.

Leech leaned closer and blinked against the shimmering video feed. "This *is* below us?"

"Yes."

"What's on the screen? That is a screen, right?"

"Yes it is. This angle is safe. If we shift to camera three you'd be able to see the screen, see what the camera is showing . . . and end up like her." Goetz tapped the corpse on screen. "You're viewing that room through a diluted feed, filtered, watered down from the experimental camera. A security precaution just in case."

"In case what?"

"In case the feed decides to shift to camera three."

Decides. Leech considered the word.

"What's on that screen?"

Tweedle Dum shuffled up behind them. "We call it backstage."

"What?"

Tweedle Dum licked his finger and dragged a trail of slime across the screen. "It's the real world."

"What the fuck are you talking about?"

"We're a goddamned TV show!" Tweedle Dee cackled. "And we're about to be cancelled!"

"Shawn!" Goetz shouted and Tweedle Dee recoiled, cheeks mottled purple. She turned to Leech. "We thought we were simply seeing into another dimension like ours. Apparently we were seeing into some kind of . . . originating space. We use the backstage metaphor for simplicity."

"Terrible name."

"How's your superstring theory?"

"Backstage it is." Leech shivered with a sudden realization. "You went there, didn't you?"

Goetz nodded, eyes wet. "Three went through." She shook her head to indicate their fate.

"The act of observation made it a door," Tweedle Dum said.

"How?"

"The Observer Effect. Observing a phenomenon changes it on a quantum level."

"You really didn't know it was a door?" Leech shook his head.

"I promise. We theorized a wave superposition state—"

His cackle interrupted her. "You people are the same every time."

"Every time?" Tweedle Dum asked. "No one has ever—"

Leech stopped him with a raised hand. "Each time, folks just like y'all say you're the first. There've been so many firsts I can't remember them all."

"Who *are* you?"

"I'm special." He aimed a finger at Goetz. "Tell me what happened."

"The Director cancelled us!" Tweedle Dee said and ran from the room, the door banging off the wall in his wake.

Tweedle Dum pointed at the ceiling. "That up there is, uh . . ." He waggled his fingertip. "This. On its way to press the off button."

"The Director? Are you telling me you sent people to meet God?"

"Not in any religious sense." Goetz shook her head. "A terribly advanced consciousness. Far beyond homo sapiens."

"And it didn't like its creations breaking free?"

"Can you imagine if Captain Kirk popped into the writers room and started complaining?" Tweedle Dum said.

"How would a TV character react to the knowledge that it was a fiction, its world a play?" Goetz added. "It's not built to confront such knowledge. It's only reaction would be unraveling. That's what's happening to everyone and everything in Durable."

"I'm not living a TV show," Leech said.

"It's just a metaphor."

"Are you saying we might be cancelling ourselves? We looked backstage, ate the fruit, lifted the curtain and did ourselves in?"

Goetz shook her head. "We don't know, just that it's happening. The fabric of our reality is fragmenting on a subatomic level." She waved at the printouts on the table. "Fictions like sanity are the first to crumble."

Leech crossed his arms as an ice pick stabbed him in the forehead. He closed his eyes against the pain.

"Outside line?" Leech pointed at the phone receiver on a wall mount.

"Press nine."

Leech hit nine and punched in the number. When Karen sighed across the miles he felt his heart melt. "Hey, honeybee."

She said a few things without quite waking up and he smiled as if she could see his face. Her voice was a song that soothed his many hurts. "Close your eyes, baby," he said at last. "Go on back to sleep."

He hung up the phone. "Take me to the camera."

10.

It looked like the control room at a recording studio with a massive engineer's deck in front of a long pane of opaque glass. "We learned to keep the window polarized," Goetz said. "Looking into the screen room without the filtering feeds . . ."

"The drive-in movie from hell."

"We had four suicides," Tweedle Dum said from a rolling chair as he pressed a series of glowing buttons. "Martense hacked the local cable before he hung himself. Fed it to the town."

Everything hurt. His ribs, his split lip, his damned teeth. Leech let it feed the low and violent flame that always smoldered in his gut. "You fools."

"Yes." Goetz touched her eyes and studied the dampness on her fingers. "I have a daughter."

Leech wasn't sure if she was apologizing or making a plea for help. The fire in his belly sent tendrils out to his limbs as a smile took hold of his face. A grin built to empty out bars and make men weak.

"Clear the window so I can see what's playing."

"You can't—"

"Do it." No raised voice. No emotion.

Goetz nodded to Tweedle Dum. "Jim, look at the back wall, don't look at the window no matter what happens." Tweedle Dum did as told, his bald head shining with sweat.

Leech inhaled through his nose and released his breath slowly as the polarized window cleared, allowing him a look at the big metal movie screen on the other side.

He saw.

He saw a universe of schizophrenia and his madness smiled in recognition. He knew it the way infants know other infants. Like minds. Like souls.

The same.

"How are you still standing?" Goetz asked.

The cancers blooming in Leech's joints were irrelevant, as were his bleeding tear ducts. Red pinpricks spotted his linen suit as he sweated out his essential vintage. If the process on the great screen continued, it would wipe away the world, expose the film, reduce reality to random code until a future reset beyond his comprehension.

There was no drug for this madness. No cosmic Clozapine to set the universal mind in order.

But Karen lived in this here. This now. That made this here and now worth keeping.

Leech moved in front of the shining metal door in the wall. A featureless thing without a handle or key pad that opened onto the screen that was a doorway.

"Open it."

"You think a fictional person can go backstage and talk to the Director?" Tweedle Dum said.

"You doubting sonofabitch. My name is Archibald Leech and I am a man of many stories." He felt mad and wonderful and motherfucking Activated.

Goetz gripped Leech's hand in both of hers. "I have a daughter." Tears made silver tracks down her cheeks. "Please."

Tweedle Dum pulled a lever and the silver door slid open with a hiss. "You can't negotiate with the Director!"

"Negotiate?" Leech looked into the strange space beyond the door where images flickered and danced on the giant screen. His bar-clearing smile stretched wide as his gums began to drip and he drew the Luger from his shoulder holster.

"They don't send me to negotiate."

THE SECOND STORY

1.

EXCERPT FROM SESSION 7 AUDIO RECORDING OF PATIENT JOHN DOE:

"What's your name?"

"Where am I?"

"Can you tell me your name?"

"My guts are turnin' over . . ."

"You were given some medication to help you relax. Do you know your name?"

Silence stretches. Cloth rustles.

"When is it?"

"When is what?"

"When is now?"

2.

EXCERPT FROM SESSION 8 AUDIO RECORDING OF PATIENT JOHN DOE:

"How are you feeling—"

"What's that red light?"

"We're recording—"

"Is that a camera? Get rid of it! Get rid of it!"

A chair clatters and words are drowned out by the sound of scuffling.

"Calm down!"

Something is smashed.

"Nurse! Clozapine, stat!"

3.

Dr. Lotz sat behind her neatly ordered desk and dragged a brush through her long, red hair, a calming ritual left over from childhood. Long fingers of wood scratched at her office windows as wind caressed the young beech tree outside, a reminder that there was life beyond the walls.

"Are you okay, Sarah?" Dr. Matthews took a seat across from her in one of two comfortable guest chairs as she hid the brush in a desk drawer. Though the office was small, Lotz had introduced her personality in the form of plants and wood and bright if amateurish photographs of woodland scenes. Matthews was one of the few who knew the photographer and what she meant to Lotz.

"I'm alright." She smiled. "He's just so skinny and passive, I let my guard down."

"Do you think it's abuse trauma? I had a young patient—"

"I mean," Lotz interrupted. "He ate up that Clozapine like it was candy and kept on struggling."

Matthews nodded and gestured. "You have dried blood on your cheek. Other cheek."

Lotz licked her fingers and rubbed at the brown line on her face. "Arnold and DeWayne are at County General with concussions. Broken bones." Lotz fixed a questioning gaze on her mentor. "Arnold played football at State. How could . . ." She shrugged.

"Lisa managed to get back some of the footage." Matthews licked his lips uneasily. "Said it was magnetized, like someone tried to wipe it."

"He didn't wipe anything, just smashed the camera and then started in on the guys."

"That's what Lisa said," Matthews continued. "Anyway, the weird thing is that even with the degraded footage I could make out both of our guys trying to subdue John Doe . . . "

"And?"

"And John Doe isn't visible on the footage."

"Not visible like he was hidden by DeWayne and Arnold? They're big."

"No. Not visible like he wasn't in the room."

4.

EXCERPT FROM SESSION 9 AUDIO RECORDING OF PATIENT JOHN DOE:

"How are you feeling?"

"It's too dark in here."

Footsteps echo and blinds rattle.

"Is that better?"

"Yes."

"Earlier you complained that it was too bright and gave you headaches. Do you remember?"

"I . . . no. There's no camera, right?"

"No cameras. We're not recording you at all. Why don't you like cameras?"

A feedback whine drowns out the patient's words until, "My head is all mixed up."

"It can take a while to find the right mix of medication."

"My belly isn't great."

"That's the sedative. Have you been on medication before?"

Silence. Papers shuffle.

"That's alright, memory can be a tricky thing. We'd like to try something to help if it's alright with you."

"What?"

"We'd like to lower your dosage and try hypnosis. Sometimes it helps patients with memory recall."

"Is this a hospital?"

"Yes."

"Why am I in a hospital?"

"We'd like you to try to remember yourself."

"My stomach . . . "
"Can we try the hypnosis?"
"Sure, I'm game."

THE THIRD STORY

1.

New Hampshire, 1952.

WE HAD PHILANDERERS, alcoholics, and communists. We had people who experimented in defiance of legal convention, intellectual thieves, and even an open homosexual. None of us fit in with the world of Doris Day and bobby socks and we were disgraced in scientific circles.

Despite that, we were all brilliant in our fields.

"Wilkes, Dick Wilkes," a man said, his hair slicked back in a ducktail, shoulders draped in a black leather jacket jangling with zippers. He looked as if he'd stepped right off the screen of a drive-in movie.

He offered his hand as we all stood about in the large, well-appointed lounge.

"Archie Leech," I said, watching his eyes for a wince of recognition.

I glanced at the abundance of tweed milling about the wet bar and the antique couches. There were beards and glasses and elbow patches aplenty.

"Listen, Archie." He paused and I nodded that using my first name was fine. "Do you know what's going on?"

I shook my head. "I received an invitation in the mail."

"Me too. Very nice calligraphy. A train ticket and a chauffeured trip in a cherry Packard. What'd they tell you?"

"It was appealing for a number of reasons," I said,

keeping the south out of my voice as much as I could. I always felt like a cracker in Yankee country when I let the grits into my voice.

"Clue me in. You think it's Uncle Sam?"

I shook my head.

He studied me and my stomach did a slow lurch, maybe he did know who I was.

"Look, I read about . . . " He hesitated and I know my expression must have gone cold because he shook his head. "Hey, no, that's not what I'm . . . look, I mean, I had my own crack up, for similar reasons."

He looked out at the high IQs operating in what was designed to be their natural element, a faculty party. "I wonder if they're all . . . "

"Disgraced?"

He nodded.

"You could ask, but it's probably taboo. Like prison."

"What do you know about prison?"

"I'm supposed to pick a fight on the first day to establish my credibility." I pointed at a wizened archaeologist named Orlov. "Him."

"Little bastard is probably a Soviet plant." Wilkes grinned and I laughed. The heads turned our way.

Wilkes grinned a lot those first few days and the work, when we found out what it was, was fascinating.

2.

The road wound across a campus of overgrown bushes and open spaces with wrought iron benches. None of the streetlights worked and what glow there was from the moon was a thin, icy thing that only served to make shadows oilier and full of movement.

I watched my penny loafers as I walked in the group, all of us clutching makeshift weapons. I'd driven nails through the end of a baseball bat and wrapped it in black electrical tape, but had no idea if I could actually swing it—

The man in front of me stopped abruptly and I ran into him.

On the road in front of us stood a small figure draped in a white sheet, like a child playing ghost.

There were no holes cut in the sheet for eyes.

A mathematician named Bonsaint said, "I can't!" and ran back the way we had come.

The wind was really snapping now and my longish hair was blowing crazily, blinding me.

"Should we rush together?" someone said.

None of us moved forward. The little figure under the sheet didn't move either.

In the end it came down to drawing straws and then I was staring down at the short straw in my hand.

"Bad luck, Archie," Wilkes said and I hated him for the relief in his voice.

I took a torch from one of the men and balanced a bat in my other hand as I stepped out from the group. My shoes slapped on the road as I crossed the empty space. There were tinny shouts of encouragement from behind me.

My feet were like lead and it seemed like miles but suddenly I was within ten feet of the diminutive wraith. The sheet crackled as it blew and I doubled over in a gut-clenching spasm that squeezed out the last dregs of bile from my belly.

"Archie!" That was Wilkes, back there. *Got your back, buddy, way back.*

I couldn't move. Couldn't lift my legs. I think I was crying but I couldn't hear my own sobs.

It would be easy. It would be as simple as hitting a kid's tee-ball.

No!

I dropped the torch and it rolled, sputtering, toward

the small shape. The sheet blew up to reveal bare legs and familiar red sneakers.

"Forgive me."

I stepped forward with a wail and swung, low and flat. I connected.

The sky ripped open with a flash of lightning and crash of thunder.

3.

The site work had to be done in complete darkness, we were told. No light at all, including ultraviolet and infrared. We practiced connecting tubes and making notes on paper that we would only be able to read when we went back to our rooms. We were allowed to speak, of course, but something about working in the absolute black pressed on us and we began to communicate by touch signals. When we did speak it was in whispers.

Information was parceled out sparingly about what we were doing and different individuals were given different directions, always by letter in our faculty mailboxes, always in elaborate calligraphy. We were instructed not to discuss the work outside our specific teams and were completely cut off from the outside world, with phone and radio contact strictly prohibited. It was paranoid even for our paranoid era.

A cabal of experimental mathematicians absorbed our reports and covered entire walls with arcane equations. Quiet speculation was our most popular sport.

Nobody knew who was delivering the letters.

"It's got to be one of us," Wilkes said, but I wasn't certain of anything.

The campus itself was surrounded by trees and very isolated. Clearly old, with brick dormitories standing empty, some speculated that it had once been a preparatory school in the old New England tradition.

Others opined that a wealthy eccentric of the Howard Hughes variety had bought all the land, interested in playing God with his own team of scientists.

None of us knew exactly where it was because we had all been picked up in the same New Hampshire town and driven into the mountains by singularly uncommunicative drivers.

And yeah, the Packard that picked me up was cherry.

What we knew for certain was that we were alone in the place. A few of the men had explored the buildings in their spare time and found them empty, some in decent repair, some decrepit and covered in mold.

My own wanderings led me into what must have been the administrative building. Faded stenciling on the window of one door said HEADMASTER, and another read only PLINE, the rest of it faded by time. I shivered at the thought of what harsh disciplines had been meted out behind that thick door, the only door not gifted with a window. I hurried on into a secretarial pool, dusty desks still equipped with rusting candlestick phones of antique make. I picked up a receiver out of curiosity but heard nothing, and the residue it left on my ear was moist and unpleasant.

The switchboard was larger than expected for a school, though the few remaining wires dangling from the board had been chewed as if by rats. I pulled one free and tossed it aside, noting the rusted pin.

"You notice that there are only fellas here?" Wilkes said later as he made two scotch and rocks at the wet bar. In his J.D. get up I expected him to smoke reefer, but Master Wilkes preferred Dewar's.

Everyone was present in the evenings after the first few days and Wilkes had a habit of seeking my company.

It wasn't a place that encouraged being alone.

"Of course," I said.

"Doesn't that strike you as odd?"

"The whole damn thing is odd."

Wilkes handed over my drink and we clinked glasses. The scotch was a warm bloom of heat as it rolled down my throat and spread throughout my chest.

"Paleobotanist and applied non-fauna ambulatory mechanics," he said, eyeing me speculatively. "An article described you as Uncle Sam's Explorer of Evolutionary What-ifs."

Old news.

"I also read your book," he said and I waited for laughter that didn't come.

The Soviets found something while developing their first nuclear reactor. Two miles beneath frozen Siberia, a lake isolated since the day the dinosaurs died. A growing concentration of unusual fossils led them to it. They resembled the great saurians of the era at first glance, but closer analysis identified anomalies. Chemical and mineral anomalies that suggested flora, not fauna.

Thanks to my security clearance, I saw it all.

I wasn't the only American to note the indications of prehistoric flora but I was the only one to posit that it represented the emergence of a new dominant predator in the Mesozoic. A new intelligence.

A vegetable intelligence.

The site shut down abruptly and Soviet state TV broadcasted images of a nuclear accident.

I wrote a book, wildly speculative I'll admit, positing that such an intelligent colony of animate plants could have retreated to a place like Lake Vostol, acclimating to the environment in order to survive the violent change on the surface. I suggested that evidence of more colonies existed. An evolutionary path that might have been.

Yggdrasil. The World Tree.

Given the right conditions, such intelligences could survive for long periods until times were ripe for re-emergence.

The book was not well-received.

"And you?" I asked, to change the subject.

"I'm the mushroom man."

"What?"

"Psilocybin," he laughed. "Studied the expanding consciousness of South American tribes." His voice boomed in an imitation of The Man. "Our boys are dying in Korea and you want funding to go where?"

"You're a damned beatnik."

He winked. "Just happy to make the scene, Daddy-O."

4.

"This is wrong . . . this is wrong," someone was saying over and over as I staggered away from the shape under the sheet and collapsed to my knees while the rain plastered my hair to my scalp and my shirt to my chest.

"Archie!" Wilkes crouched next to me, zippers jangling. "You're gonna be okay, pal, you're gonna be okay."

He held out my bat and I recoiled, but took it in one shaky hand.

"This is wrong," somebody moaned.

I shook my head.

"You had to do it," Wilkes said.

"It felt goddamned strange. It didn't feel like I hit a skull at all. It was more like . . . I mean, I think the head came right off but I couldn't see."

I glanced over at the knot of men staring down at the dead thing while they screwed up their courage to lift the sheet.

"It was a helluva swing," Wilkes said. He offered a flask and I took a healthy belt, coughing at the harsh burn.

There was a sudden commotion and then someone screamed, "Oh Christ, it's moving!"

The men scattered as the form beneath the sheet staggered upright. Something round rolled away and out of the torch light.

"Kill it! Someone kill it!" Soames shrieked.

A man rushed forward and swung a rake, the metal tines punching through fabric and lodging in whatever was beneath. The figure whirled away drunkenly and the man let go of his rake, which stayed stuck in the thing.

"How can it move without a head?" Wilkes was looking at it wide-eyed and it might have been the rain but I thought he had pissed his pants.

"You seem to have lost your happy place, my friend," I said to Wilkes and he backed away from whatever was in my eyes. I whirled towards the thing and saw that its sheet was sliding off and thought that if I really saw the headless child's body beneath I would go completely mad.

"Burn it!" I screamed at the scattering men. "Burn it, you chickenshit motherfuckers!"

But their courage was broken and they backed away, dropping their makeshift weapons.

I grabbed Wilkes by the shoulder and shoved him towards the group. "Burn it!"

When I saw that Wilkes had understood, I turned back and threw the bat with all my strength.

The weapon arced through the rain and bounced across the road, and the headless thing stumbled in its direction. A small, red sneaker came down hard on the nails driven into the wood. It tried to take another step but the bat was stuck in its foot and it tripped.

"Get it, Wilkes! Beat feet!" I screamed, my voice going hoarse.

Wilkes charged like a broken field runner, a satchel clutched to his chest. He skidded to a stop and heaved the satchel, which burst against the writhing form, spreading the gelatin our chemists had made.

He scooped up a guttering torch and threw it.

For a moment nothing happened and I thought the wet had killed the flame. Then fire bloomed with an audible noise, magnesium bright.

5.

I shut the canvas flap behind me, feeling around in the dark for the knob. Stepping through the door, I probed with my foot for the first step down and closed the door behind me.

I found the safety line and followed the rope down the stairs, my eyes open for purely psychological reasons. I had initially thought that keeping my eyes closed would make working in the dark more natural, but it made me uneasy.

At first those of us on the physical science team had used the basement of the faculty building as a practice space, learning to work in the dark. When the team was ready, we converted the basement into our blackout laboratory and nobody else was allowed entry.

There was a tug on the line and I knew someone was down here with me the way a spider knows a fly is in its web. I tugged back.

I reached an intersection of cords and felt for three knots, then followed that line, my feet scraping in a shuffle-step across the gritty floor.

I could smell it as I got closer. Damp and mealy and somehow familiar. I was distantly aware that the smell had grown since my last visit. When my hand felt three more knots I knelt down carefully and pulled several vials from the pack on my belt.

Despite the setting, it wasn't unlike the work I had done for the government in the days before my book. The Soviets had a vast and vulnerable breadbasket, grain fields and factory farms without which they'd starve. The US of A wanted to know what would happen if, say, wheat stalks could be cross-pollinated with other plants to emit toxic spores. What wind patterns would blow it to what cities.

Drive the citizens of Vladivostok mad?

Deprive the population of Irkutsk of sleep until they collapsed from exhaustion?

It was good work, godlike in the Shiva sense of the word. Until we received the intelligence about Lake Vostol.

Until I discovered the World Tree and wrote the book.

I sneezed and returned to the task at hand.

Using the size of the vials to tell me the order of application, I used an eyedropper to drip the liquid from each into the mouths of three separate copper tubes. I then removed another small bottle and dripped an enzyme found in the brains of octopi into the mouth of the center tube.

I heard a moist swelling sound from the darkness in front of me and paused. A terrible curiosity made me want to reach out and touch whatever the tubes were feeding.

My hand stretched forward tentatively and the smell intensified.

Something brushed my shoulder.

"It is Orlov," he said before I could scream.

Breath whooshed from my lungs and I stood, perspiration beading my forehead.

The instructions had been very explicit and touching whatever the tubes led too was strictly verboten.

"Let there be light," Orlov said. "One wonders how we would experience creation if denied our sense of sight."

It was eerie having a conversation in the pitch dark. I felt as if I were standing in the midst of an invisible crowd.

"I'm done here." I slipped past Orlov on the rope and followed it back to the stairs.

He had appeared just as I was about to violate the instructions. I wondered what his tasking was, down in the basement. Scientist or sentry?

As I reached the top of the stairs I realized what I had smelled where no light was allowed. The scent of a memory from childhood.

My grandmother canned tomatoes in her dirt-walled cellar. I had once crept down into the dark underground space to break the seal on a single container. I was curious how long the tomatoes would last without her special alchemy. It was six months before we visited again and I returned to the cellar to carefully remove a tomato from the unsealed jar. The tomato was soft and bloated to the touch. The skin seemed to move around the body of the fruit when I pressed my finger against it. I knew what a tomato felt like and at an intuitive level, understood that the swollen globe I was examining had become something else, something new. Unable to help myself, I pressed my finger deeper into the tomato, dimpling it until the skin swelled up around my finger to the end of my fingernail, as if it was absorbing me. Soon my finger was embraced by the fruit to the depth of my first knuckle. Faster than my senses could communicate, the skin parted and a white mass boiled out of the hole to spatter against my hand. The stench that puffed out in a wave struck like a physical blow, somewhere past fruit and flesh and into a level of putrescence that was its own definable category.

That is what I smelled in the basement.

6.

"We have to look for the head."

"You look for the fucking head!"

The gelatin was still burning in a wide puddle and the rain hissed into steam as it poured down. The men were edging back into a group, or maybe just into the circle of firelight.

"My bat," I said, gesturing listlessly at the fire.

"We'll get you another bat." They seemed a little afraid of me.

"Here it is!" That was Feinman.

"Oh my fucking lord," someone else responded, I wasn't sure whom.

I started over but Wilkes stopped me. "Better not."

Picking up a torch, I wandered away while they

exclaimed in loathing laced with an undercurrent of the scientist's awful fascination. Wilkes was using a rake to slide it towards the fire.

I looked out into the rain while they burned my daughter's head behind me.

7.

Wilkes put a record on the turntable in the lounge and bopped his head in time with Fats Domino.

"Turn off that negro music," Soames bellowed.

Wilkes froze mid bop before swiveling on his heel to face the taller, much fatter man.

"Say that again, pops."

Mottled pink spread across Soames' jowls but he wanted no part of the younger man's glittering smile.

When the crowd of stuffed shirts shuffled off to their end of the room Wilkes laid a hand on my shoulder and leaned in close.

"You heard about Betty, right?"

The man in question, a pre-Cambrian specialist, bore the last name of Davis. Naturally, Wilkes had christened him Betty and the unfortunate nickname had caught on.

"I heard him shouting last night," I said, taking the scotch Wilkes handed me.

Poor Betty's mind had snapped and he was caught running through the halls screaming about a visit from his wife. His dead wife.

"Excuse me."

We both looked up from where we had hunkered in our spot by the fireplace. It was Jeffs, the professor deemed unfit by Catholic educators.

"Do you mind if I join you?"

Wilkes patted the cushion. "Sit."

Joining our little group was something of a departure for Jeffs. Academic caste systems are rigid and Jeffs had been a small satellite orbiting Soames. Joining the outliers was a step down by most lights.

As the Beats would say, we were, "Radioactive."

"Sing, brother." Wilkes said. "Why the long face?"

I studied the man's waxen pallor. "You look terrified."

Jeffs was rubbing his glasses obsessively on his shirt and sweat was beading on his upper lip.

"You know about Betty last night?"

"He said his wife paid him a midnight visit."

Jeffs nodded and pressed his lips together. I thought he was about to cry.

"Out with it, man," Wilkes said and Jeffs shrunk in on himself.

"Hey." I leaned closer. "What is it?"

"I saw Mark last night!" He hissed. "He was looking in the window, just staring in at me. He was—he wasn't wearing any clothes."

"Who's Mark?" I asked, and Jeffs unloaded everything in a rush. I don't think he paused to take a breath. Mark was his first love. Jeffs thought about him all the time and when he'd get stuck in life he would ask *What would Mark do?* the way some people ask about Jesus.

Mark had died when Jeffs was sixteen.

"I didn't want to tell Soames. I don't want to be sedated like Betty."

"You dream about him?" I asked and Jeffs nodded. I'd been having dreams as well. Dreams of my daughter.

Wilkes scratched his chin. "The Hota people were dream thieves. They used psilocybin to—" He stopped when Feinman ran into the room like a living record scratch.

"Betty's gone!"

"Impossible," Soames said, rising ponderously. "I gave him enough sedative to knock out a horse."

"Yeah, well, he's not in his room."

The group moved in a noisy herd up the stairs to the

residential quarters and if it had been a crime scene we would have destroyed the evidence.

"This is impossible," Soames said, blocking the doorway to the empty bedroom.

"Get bent," Wilkes said.

Soames gave him a look that had wilted many an undergrad. He started to say something but Wilkes stepped into his space and the older man backed up.

I pushed into the room and breathed in the damp, mealy smell.

"What is it, Archie?"

I saw a puddle on the ground near the unlatched window. There were several wet spots on the floor leading from the windowsill to the bed.

8.

"I don't know if it's wise to carry both a satchel and a torch, Leech," Soames said, looking more ridiculous than the rest of us with his sopping wet hair and waterlogged tweed.

I gave him a sickly grin and pictured my daughter, who had died ten years ago in a drunk driving accident with me at the wheel.

"Who are you going to see, Soames?"

The fat man turned away without answering.

Jeffs touched my arm. "He's right, Archie."

The slight man's glasses had fogged over in the rain and his eyes were unreadable but I let him take the flammable satchel and started walking, lifting the torch. I knew he would follow me. He had grit. Wilkes, too.

They all followed me. We had five torches now and four satchels. The chemists had done their work well and the satchels would burn with vigor.

"You okay?" Wilkes said to Jeffs.

"I'm scared," Jeffs replied. "Mark is out here somewhere. I don't think I can . . . to him."

I barely noticed his words as I relived the feeling of taking a baseball bat to my daughter's head, the strange shock that traveled up the wood and into my arms, the sensation that it felt *wrong* . . . as if there was a right feeling to braining your daughter.

"It won't really be Mark," I said.

9.

"There isn't a flashlight in this entire goddamned place." Wilkes slammed a cabinet shut.

Jeffs appeared with a dozen candles and several candelabras cradled awkwardly.

"No lights down in the basement. The rules were very explicit on that," Soames said. "You'll destroy the experiment."

"To quote Socrates, fuck a bunch of experiments," Wilkes said.

I forced a smile, but my head was buzzing with impossibilities. It was one thing to theorize in my Georgetown office, but here, in the dark, it was another thing entirely.

We went out and around to the back of the building where the canvas blackout tent protected the basement entrance. It was late afternoon but we still had gray sunlight leaking through the clouds.

"Gonna storm soon," Wilkes said.

I handed my candelabra to Jeffs and grabbed the canvas flap, then paused.

"Anybody seen Orlov lately?" I asked. Both men shook their heads.

Bracing one foot against the wall, I heaved backward and the blackout tent fell with a crash.

"You can't do this," Soames called out as the rest of the men approached in a herd with the big professor at their head.

"Just watch us," Wilkes called back and the entire

group of them halted so as not to be tainted by the actions of a few bad apples.

"This is—" Soames began and I pivoted on my heel, snatching a candelabra from Jeffs.

"What, blasphemy?" Laughing humorlessly, I looked around at the lot of us as man after man found the ground a fascinating study. "We're certainly experts in that field, every one of us."

I twisted the doorknob and opened it. A waft of fetid air exhaled from the dark maw of the basement workspace.

"Oh crap," Wilkes muttered behind me as I stepped inside and flicked the wheel on a lighter, bringing flame to the wicks of my candles. They guttered as the wet air resisted them, but I waited until they had grown strong and reached for the guide rope leading down the stairs.

My hand grasped empty air.

No matter. I held the candelabra out before me.

In the flickering light I noticed that the guide rope lay discarded on the stairs, but didn't consider the implications in my eagerness to actually see what we had done in the workspace. The scientist in me tingled like a boy about to receive his first kiss.

My foot stepped from wood to dirt and I raised the candelabra over my head. Even so feeble a light offended the darkness and it gave way enough for my engorged pupils to rip aside the glamour.

"What is it?" Jeffs said from behind me.

"What's the hold up?" Wilkes called from further up the stairs.

I turned and candle wax popped. Jeffs backed up one step. I was sure my eyes were solid masses of black, the pupils expanding to eat both sclera and light.

"It's gone," I said hoarsely. "There's nothing here."

Jeffs pointed.

"What's that?"

We gathered around his horrible discovery.

10.

I brushed the sopping hair from my eyes to see a flash of white movement.

"Look over there!"

"Why are they covering themselves in sheets?" Jeffs stepped closer as the group followed some deeply inscribed instinct to circle and face outward.

"Maybe they don't like the rain," Feinman said.

"I think it's light," Wilkes said. "It's our torches."

"Come on," I said, shivering and cold like every bedraggled one of us.

The main school buildings humped up out of the darkness in front of us. Old stone things with narrow halls and deep cellars according to what Betty, Slattery, and Heller had said. The three men had been the most intrepid of our campus explorers before they went missing and were the only men to have visited the old buildings.

Conclusive? Of course not. But the buildings were as far from our workspace and living area as one could be and still remain on campus.

"Archie, you sure—"

"Yes. And you are, too."

"I'm seeing more of them," Wilkes added, glancing back. "Hey, who's leaving the group?"

A torch, its bearer indistinct, was moving off the path and onto the grounds.

"Who is that?"

There was a bright flash accompanied by a sharp crack and the torch tumbled to the ground.

I stepped onto the grass and walked towards the dark lump beside the still-burning torch. One thing you can say about a group of scientists, we make fine torches.

"Who is it?" a voice said from the safety of the walkway as I knelt and held my flame high over the corpse. "Who?"

The dead man's head was strangely deflated and his once pompous features were as grotesque and unsympathetic in death as I had found them in life. A revolver gleamed in the grass near his hand.

"Who did you see?" I whispered to the corpse, picking up the weapon.

"Holy shit, where did Soames get a gun?" Wilkes said.

A fluttering white sheet darted from one hedge to the next. I lifted the revolver and pulled the trigger, the flash blinding, explosion deafening. When my vision cleared there was nothing but empty space.

I attempted to stand and my knee dug a groove through the muddy lawn instead. Hands caught me beneath the armpits and helped me upright.

"Thanks."

Wilkes dragged a wet sleeve across his mouth, looking at Soames. "When my ex-wife shows up, you let me borrow that, okay?"

II.

I tilted my empty glass and watched as the ice slid around the inside. The debate raged around me in the faculty lounge but I took no part.

"They're teeth!" Jeffs shouted.

"They are no such—" Soames began and I glanced over as Wilkes lifted the thing we had found in the basement.

"One, two, three teeth," Wilkes said. "Human molars to be exact."

I shivered, remembering the warm slipperiness of the object when I picked it up from the basement floor.

"Do you know what you're suggesting?"

Clink. The diminishing ice made another circuit around the bottom of my glass. A small sound escaped my throat but nobody heard. My gut was hollow. My soul ash.

"What have we done?" I said and Wilkes whipped around toward me, seeking an ally.

I looked over the group, waiting for me to weigh in. "Where is Slattery?" I said and heads turned, murmurs rising in a wave of sound. "First Betty and now Slattery are missing. And what about Heller?" I deliberately left out Orlov, my thoughts about him already metastasizing into certainty. "And I know of two more people who saw . . ." Jeffs shot me a pleading glance. "Things," I finished. "Has anyone else been visited?"

I stared at a sea of expressionless masks and sipped at my drink. The ice bounced off my teeth.

"When was the last time anyone received an envelope? They were coming fast and furious even two days ago."

Heads shook. Murmuring coarsened in tone, leavened with fear.

"We've made the thing we were meant to make. Performed our function." I paused, adrift in my personal shame. "Now we've been discarded. Deservedly so."

"Wait a minute—"

"If someone was going to silence us, they would have already come!"

"Why? When they can just leave us here to be picked off by . . . what we've unleashed."

Feinstein pushed his way into the group, face flushed. The normally reticent scientist was visibly shaken. "I tried to fix the phones. You know, the old switchboard we found—"

"Yes," Soames said, asserting dominance.

"They're not just old and used up. They've been deliberately disabled. Recently disabled."

"You mean you can't—"

"I was trying, but I heard something coming. I beat feet, fellas. There was no way I was staying there alone."

I walked the perimeter of the room, the group shuffling as it turned to follow my passage. "This is why we were selected, you self-aggrandizing jackasses. Did you think it was because we're brilliant? Because we deserve a second chance?"

My laugh was a sickening croak.

"We're perfect. Willing to do anything to get back into the game. And disposable."

"It really isn't Uncle Sam, is it?" Wilkes asked.

"I'm sorry, Dick, this is something else entirely."

"Who is it? Who brought us here?"

How to explain my theory without sounding mad, even after what they'd seen?

"Archie, why don't you sit down?" Soames said before ducking nimbly to one side. My whiskey glass shattered on the far wall.

Cowards, I could see them retreating from yet another burden of guilt.

Jeffs moved to my side, tears slipping from his eyes. "Archie is right. You know he's right."

"Too late to undo it," Wilkes said.

"We should leave," Feinstein said. "Now."

"Leave how?" Wilkes laughed. "There are no cars. No phones. How far can you walk? How about Soames?"

"Hey—" Soames began but I interrupted him.

"This has happened before, a new intelligence asserting itself. But homo sapiens wasn't there to stop it last time."

"What—"

"We were tricked into bringing it back and Wilkes is right. It's too late to undo that."

I stepped forward and the men parted around me. There, on the table, rested the gray thing I had pulled from the basement. I picked it up and my skin crawled at the touch. I could feel my lips peeling back from my teeth.

"But not too late to destroy it," I said, closing my hand into a fist. The thing resisted for a moment and then collapsed inward, fibrous, fleshy strands squeezing out from between my fingers. Teeth rained down onto the wooden table top like miniature dice. Someone sobbed and ran from the room but I didn't look up.

Outside, a gust of wind rattled the large windows looking out over the dark campus.

There were a thousand questions still to be asked but Wilkes waved them all aside. "Two hours. Everyone who can, meet back here in two hours. And I think we need to prepare some weapons."

Wilkes' voice trailed off as I approached the window, the sound of bouncing teeth still sharp in my ears. I could feel myself becoming unmoored. For a moment the recurring shame had filled me, but now, spent, my heart was a bladder squeezed empty of emotion.

"Archie? Archie?"

I ignored the voice as my daughter danced through my memory.

12.

Lightning flashed and a tree exploded into flame not fifty feet away. The immediate clap of thunder nearly drove me to my knees.

A lone figure waited for us on the broad, stone steps of the main campus building.

"Archie," Wilkes said. "The fellas are hot-rodding."

I shrugged off his hand, ears still ringing. I thought I recognized the one who waited for us.

"Get back here, you cowards," Wilkes shouted as I lifted the torch.

Orlov hunched atop the steps, shivering in the torrential downpour. There was a horrible rip in the skin over his cheek and I thought I could make out the white of bone.

"How d-d-do you say n-n-no to God?" Orlov said through chattering teeth.

"What did we do?" I asked.

Orlov looked down on me with an expression of such torment I almost felt sympathy.

"It's remaking itself n-n-ow," he said. "Learning from its children. From you." He recoiled as the double doors behind him boomed open. White forms glided out from the dark opening, their sheets immediately plastered to their figures by the downpour.

"I'm sorry, I'm sorry," Orlov wailed as the figures in white formed a circle around him on the stairs, taking no notice of us.

"Nooooo," the little man screamed as a dozen hands dragged him into the dark interior of the building. Screams rolled out to us like the tolling of a bell.

"They're coming out of the trees," a quiet voice said.

There were only four of us left. Wilkes and Jeffs, of course. But Feinman was a surprise.

"Mark?" Jeffs said but I kept my eyes on the dark doorway as a scuffle ensued behind me. "It's not Mark!" Wilkes shouted. I heard the slap of running feet and the sound of a fight.

"Light it," Feinman said. "Don't look!"

A bright flare of light washed over me and cast my shadow hugely across the front of the stone building. Eerie wailing sounded from all around us.

"They can't stand the light!" Wilkes shouted as I picked up Jeffs' fallen satchel.

What do you say to God?

I ascended the stairs, slinging the satchel over my shoulder to free my hands for torch and revolver.

My footsteps echoed in the hall as I entered the building. Inside, the mealy smell was nauseating and I waved my torch ahead of me in an effort to disperse it.

A black trail of blood guided me forward. I stepped over jumbles of familiar copper tubing and broken glass beakers taken from our workspace. They had been busy.

I saw movement as I passed a junction of corridors and fired quickly in both directions. My ears rang from the noise and when I looked again the corridors were empty.

Two bullets remained in the pistol.

The stench intensified as I headed downstairs past a sign denoting the Theater and Assembly Area. A big space, I thought. Windowless and dark. I could hear a hundred voices whispering.

Quiet footsteps sounded on the stairs behind me but I ignored them.

The doors to the theater itself were heavy wooden things and windowless. I slipped the pistol into my belt and pulled open the righthand door, thrusting my torch through the opening. Movement erupted and I had the sense of many bodies retreating before the light.

When I judged the entry clear, I stepped through.

The odor was overpowering and I gagged, the scientist in me noting that the alchemy of the place was wrong. The amount of oxygen and carbon dioxide altered. My torch bloomed wildly, devouring the fuel as I looked down the rows of seats into the blackness of the stage. All around me was movement as pale forms shrank back.

One hand over my mouth, I stumbled down the sloped aisle. The darkness shifted on the stage and I had the sense of something huge lurking in the depths.

I tripped twice before reaching the first row of seats. My head was spinning. The chemicals fueling my fire were nearly consumed and it was no more than a candle flame when I bumped against the lip of the stage and laboriously pulled myself up.

I shrugged the satchel strap off my shoulder and slid it before me like an offering.

The darkness shifted and whispers surrounded me, aided by the acoustics of the stage. The sense of something bloated was overwhelming and I slid my flickering torch across the boards into the deep black.

I beheld Yggdrasil.

"Oh my God."

A hundred mouths whispered back, "Oh my God."

The World Tree was God imagined as a mushroom. A vast toadstool with a blistered stem of greater diameter than the greatest redwood. Its vast cap was the soft red of peeled flesh and drooped hugely over the stage, pulsing as it consumed the atmosphere. But it was the gills slashed into the underside of the cap that wrenched a strangled scream from my throat. Great lines scoring an acre of pale flesh like the doughy underside of a fat man's arm.

My torch flared brightly and I saw the myriad eyes blinking from between the gills like bright fish in deep sea caverns. Some blue, some brown, others milky with cataracts.

Yggdrasil was acclimating to its new environment.

Eons ago it had absorbed Basidiomycota to live in the lightless subterranean world. An exercise of mycology suggesting a science far beyond our own.

Now the World Tree was absorbing us to live in our world. Weaving us into one giant, whispering and weeping thing.

My torch finally went out, its tip reduced to a blue glow. In the darkness I heard the sound of something soft and unimaginably heavy dragging itself across the wooden stage until it was close enough to touch.

I pressed my face into cool flesh and began to eat.

THE FOURTH STORY

1.

"MY NAME IS ARCHIBALD," the patient said, relief evident on his face. He was wan and drawn, shaved skull sporting new bristles, his body frightfully thin beneath his hospital gown. His pupils were fat with drugs and the dark circles beneath his eyes looked like the aftermath of a beating. Paper-thin skin stretched over the points of his cheekbones and Dr. Lotz fought the temptation to press against those points until they poked through.

"Archibald, I have something to show you," Lotz said, pulling her hair back and slipping an elastic band around it to make a ponytail. "Do you feel up to a short trip?"

"Outside?" The patient turned towards the venetian blinds covering the window. The narrow circles of his nostrils quivered. "I'd enjoy some air."

"Come with me."

2.

Leech blinked behind oversized sunglasses borrowed from one of the nurses, craning his head this way and that to take in the manicured grounds and the forbidding rise of the hospital. In his fevered imagination it towered like an insect, the windows gleaming like a thousand eyes.

"It's a very old building," Dr. Lotz noted as she pushed him across the parking lot in a wheelchair.

"There's a fence." He gestured at the black iron barrier encircling the grounds. He wore socks and slippers, bare shins chilled by the cool October air. He shivered despite the grey cardigan—one of Lotz's own sweaters—but seemed otherwise happy to be outdoors, even in a parking lot.

"Yes," she said. "The place was designated a historical site and we were able to restore the original iron fence."

He laughed and aimed a trembling finger at a house overlooking the facility from atop a neighboring hill. It was tall, gabled and gothic and struck him as a fiction.

"What is that?" His smile was faint but present.

"The Director's Residence, erected when the hospital was first built." They stopped beside a spit-shined BMW. "See anything you recognize?"

"In the parking lot?"

She nodded.

"The air is so sweet."

"Yes. Let's get you in the car."

The drive was long but quiet, the BMW gliding around curves and down country lanes lined with trees. Leggy eastern rosebuds and yellow honey locusts. A loblolly pine stood green against the fading colors of its deciduous cousins and Leech wondered about the depth of his arboreal knowledge. He noted that the honey locust leaves had not truly changed colors and knew he was not in the northeast. He enjoyed this ability to think, to recognize things, and decided he didn't want any more pills.

The car rocked over a pothole and the patient grimaced. Maybe a few pills for the pain.

They had plastic bottles of water that crinkled in his hand and sandwiches made of cucumber and goat cheese between slices of dry bread, wrapped neatly in plastic sandwich bags. "Did your husband make these?"

"I'm unmarried."

"No ball and chain?"

Lotz shook her head again. "And you?"

Confusion twisted his features and he looked away, rolling down the window with the press of a button. He closed his eyes and lost himself in the rushing wind.

Sunlight sparkled on the windshield, sliding across the glass to warm the patient's arm as they rounded a corner onto a lane between fields where great plants displayed broad green leaves. Every cell in his body was infected with pain but his clearing mind noted Sol's changing position and knew they were heading south.

"Where are we?"

"It's better if you can remember on your own." Loose hairs danced around her head in an auburn corona. "We're only fifty miles or so from where we found you."

"Found me?"

Lotz went silent.

"We're in the south," the patient said.

"Why do you say that?"

"It's not a memory, if that's what you're asking." He jerked his chin at the passing fields. "Tobacco isn't farmed anywhere else."

Lotz flicked a surprised glance at him. "What does that tell you?"

"I want a cigarette?"

Lotz allowed a smile. "About yourself. What do your observations tell you about yourself."

Leech closed his eyes and relaxed his features. "I see things."

"You're very observant."

The patient opened his eyes. "Were there bars on the windows at the hospital?"

Lotz tilted her head to the side in a gesture the patient didn't understand.

"That hospital . . . is it a psychiatric hospital?"

"Belmont Psychiatric Hospital," Lotz said. "Does that suggest anything to you?"

"Oh man." He pressed the heels of his hands against his eyes. "I'm a loony bird?"

Lotz returned her gaze to the road. The patient didn't seem to notice southern lilt that was creeping into his speech.

3.

The tombstones rose from a well-manicured hill, casting long shadows as the sun slid down the western sky. Fallen leaves rustled and danced in the breeze and Lotz pulled her BMW to a stop inside the ornate iron gate, setting the emergency brake before turning off the engine.

"Do you feel up to a short walk?"

"You're not planning to bury me, are you, doc?"

She smiled. "Of course not."

Leech pushed open his door and stood unsteadily, hands braced on the car. He shivered as the wind plucked at his gown and touched his head as if to settle a hat.

Lotz circled the vehicle and took the patient's arm to steady him. "Are you alright?"

"I'll admit I'm afraid, ma'am."

"I'm right here with you."

He thought that wasn't exactly the same thing as saying there was nothing to fear, but decided he was at the cemetery to learn and not to work his jaw, so he stayed quiet.

They shuffled through grass and leaves, pausing when he grew short of breath. Most of the flowers left at various markers were dried and curled, so the patient surmised it was several days since Sunday last. He was appreciating the musty smell of leaves and clean odor of grass. Woodsmoke came to him from an unseen house sporting a fireplace. All of it was much nicer than the urine and chemical stink of the hospital, an odor he had been largely unaware of until he escaped it.

Escape.

The word tap-danced behind his eyes and held an invisible finger across his lips. It was not a word that wanted to be shared.

Up the hill they went like an old couple, though neither was beyond middle age and Leech was wondering why he would want to escape medical attention that he clearly needed when Dr. Lotz said, "We're here."

The good doctor adjusted a knee-length skirt and knelt, brushing dead leaves from a granite marker set into the ground, a humble thing that loomed large in the patient's mind and struck him with terror.

"I don't want to look."

"I need you to see this."

"Read it to me."

"Open your eyes and read it yourself."

He lowered his chin and rubbed water from his eyes, reading the name cut into the grey stone.

"Oh no." His knees went weak and he wound up seated on the grass with a hand over his eyes.

"What does it say?" she asked in a soft voice.

"Archibald Leech," he said. "It says Archibald Leech is buried right beneath where I'm sitting."

"Tell me what year the stone says he was buried."

Leech propped himself on a hand and leaned over the marker, moving his lips as he read, spots of color blooming on his cheeks. He blew out a big breath. "1952."

"Seven decades ago," she said, studying the patient's face.

He looked at his hands, nicked and scarred and bony, but not an old man's hands. "The memories were so clear. How can that be?"

"Can you remember anything else about Archibald Leech?"

A gust of wind sent a swirl of leaves around the patient as if he was the center of a storm.

"It takes time," she said, sitting back on her heels to pluck a leaf from her hair. "We'll get there." She flicked a glance at the sky. "I don't like the look of those clouds."

The patient lifted his eyes to the darkening sky and tears carved mercury trails down his face. "Well, shit."

4.

The rain crashed down with sudden violence and Dr. Lotz cursed herself for not checking the weather reports. Thunder cracked overhead as if a giant had clapped his hands and she flinched. She steadied her hands on the wheel and slowed as the downpour consumed the illumination from her headlights, diminishing their range to mere feet.

When she glanced at the patient she was startled to see the emerald gleam of his eyes fixed on her, reflecting the unsettling green of the dashboard lights.

"Trouble's coming," he said a moment before the roar of an engine filled their world. A blue van without lights materialized from the storm behind them and clipped the BMW's rear bumper, spinning the smaller car off the road.

5.

The men of violence were a matched set with thick shoulders and scarred hands. They pulled dimestore Halloween masks over their faces and snapped the elastic bands into place before shoving their way out of the midnight blue van and splashing across the road towards the red glow of the BMW's taillights.

Nightmare faces swam into Leech's view as the passenger door was yanked open. Blue sparks flashed as a taser locked his muscles tighter than a drum. Before he could uncoil from his clench, a needle punched into the straining tendons on his neck and one of the violent men dragged him out of the car and up the muddy slope of the ditch. He was unconscious by the time his flopping body was rolled into the back of the van.

Dr. Lotz was pressing a palm against her throbbing forehead when her door was wrenched open. A thick hand grabbed a fistful of her hair and dragged her face-first into the mud. She choked, coughing slop from her mouth and trying to lift her head when a demonic green face filled her vision. Before she could scream, she felt a sharp sting at the base of her skull.

Her consciousness spread apart and dissolved as liquid valium found the GABA receptors in her brain and flipped the off switch.

FIRST INTERLUDE

1.

LEECH SAT UP in the dark, startled awake by a wet sound and the thunder of angry growling. The room was bathed in faint starlight and his bare chest was dappled with sweat, his legs covered in light pajama pants of a style that was familiar to him from black and white TV shows.

He flinched at a new sound and realized that the racket was caused by the woman sleeping by his side. Had he blacked out after a night on the town, only to awaken in a stranger's bed?

Padding across a shag rug to the dark maw of a bathroom, he tried to shake off the cobwebs. He managed to close the door by feel and find a light switch by running his fingers across the damp tiles of a wall.

The sink was deep and white and the water that splashed from the faucet was delightfully cold. He cupped his hands and drank like a bachelor before splashing his face and wiping the gummy sleep sand from his eyes.

His reflection spoke of Buchenwald and only the fact that it was in color told him he wasn't looking at old newsreel footage. The scarecrow in the mirror was indeed himself, slat ribbed with sharply drawn clavicles and a ghoulish face. He rubbed water over the stubble on his scalp and wondered what possessed him to shave himself so. It looked horrible. Beads of water nestled in between the spiky hairs like jewels and he shook his head until they flew free to speckle the mirror.

An alarm chimed in his mind, a minor thing more doorbell than siren. He had a vague sense of having felt poor of late, but no concrete memories of what had ailed him. Recent events didn't so much elude his grasping memory as fail to exist at all.

Instinct told him to pause and allow his eyes to adjust after he turned off the light. Quiet steps took him back into the bedroom and he studied the snoring woman, bathed blue by night. Was she married? Was there a husband who owned the pants he wore, an angry fellow who might appear with a shotgun in his fist?

He slipped from the room like an eddy of wind and ghosted down a narrow hallway towards a carpeted staircase that led downstairs towards what appeared to be the front door of the house.

Keen ears picked out the ticking of a grandfather clock that stood like a tall shadow in the corner of a living room, the pale clock face too eerily human for his liking. All the sounds had an odd, muffled quality, as if the walls were built with acoustic baffling.

Beside the front door was a window with a plastic shade and he eased it aside, careful that it didn't clatter up and awake the woman above. He made out the dark expanse of a front lawn with a road at the far edge. There were trees across the road and he couldn't see any other houses from his vantage point, nor could he make out a car in the driveway.

He slipped from the window as if trying not to startle a deer. Quiet across a polished wooden floor and past a small dining room table, paced by his reflection in the glass of a china cabinet.

The kitchen showed the first sign of disarray, his nose detecting the stink of dead coffin nails before he spied the ceramic ashtray on the table. Two empty wine bottles gave off the sour reek of rancid grapes. Instinct sent him to the wooden knife block on the counter where the handle of a carving knife found his grip. It commended his selection with a metallic hiss when he drew it forth.

The blade traced a steel arc through the air as if it had seen movement before he did. The thing squatted beside a coffee maker on a counter, square and ugly in the way of older appliances, the movement nothing more than his reflection shimmering across the curved glass screen.

Perspiration on his chest froze into beads of ice. He felt his vision tunneling towards the old TV and before he knew what he was doing, he snatched it from the counter and tucked it under one arm as he dashed like a running back across the thick shag carpeting of the living room, spying an even larger television hunched amidst an entertainment center complete with stereo and bronze trophies and—

He was at the front door, the knife between his teeth as he wrenched at the knob and hurried outside across the dewy grass. The TV was lifted over his head in both hands and thrown hard against the lawn, where it bounced unsatisfactorily. But time was of the essence and he spun back to the house, his vision still tunneled so that seeing was like swinging an old telescope. Back to the door he loped and in seconds had hooked his hands behind the living room television and wrenched it from its moorings. Cords whipped his skin as it bounced and jangled across the rug and he kept it moving by crouching and throwing his weight against it. Lifting and heaving the heavy monstrosity until it banged down the front steps with a happy clatter of plastic and glass.

It slid like a tackling dummy across the grass until it was beside its smaller brother. If he was wearing shoes he would have kicked it. Instead he ran to the garage on the assumption that trimmed grass meant a lawn mower, which meant a gas can.

The garage door clattered up and he stepped into the garage, seeing no car but wary of slipping on oil stains, using his clever nose to find a gas can. It sloshed as he carried it back to the television graveyard on the front lawn.

He flicked the knife point into the lawn and rushed to the house. A light went on upstairs but he paid it no mind as he rifled the kitchen drawers with little effort at discretion. He had the sense that time was growing short even as a woman's voice called down the stairs.

Matches! He snatched up the box and dashed back outside, skidding and nearly falling as he reached the televisions. Gas gurgled from the can as if it was eager to help him burn these fuckers to the ground.

The first match snapped against the striking pad on the side of the box but the second flared to life, the sharp stink of sulphur burning his nostrils. A flick sent the tiny meteor flaming towards its target and set the devices alight, flame whooshing high as he stepped back, noticing then that the hem of his right pant leg was smoldering.

Fearing that he had splashed gas on himself, he knelt and dragged the afflicted shin through the grass and was pausing to assess the effect when running footsteps and bobbing flashlights drew his attention to the road.

"What the hell are you doing?" a man's voice snarled.

"Burning TVs," Leech shot back.

"What?"

"Are you blind as well as stupid?" He snatched up the carving knife. "I'm burning the damn TVs."

"Drop the weapon," a new voice said, more gravelly than the first.

"Drop the knife," the first man said as the two separated. Leech gained a sense of their size and thought that they each outweighed him to the tune of a hundred pounds.

He didn't like the slippery feel of the grass beneath his feet and had decided to take the fight to them on the road when an ear-splitting shriek dopplered by as the woman ran past wearing nothing more than a pair of thin panties.

Instinct sent his free arm out like a clothesline. He wrapped it around her waist, using her momentum to spin around and deposit her on the grass. She took two stumbling steps towards the house before realizing that her coordinates were off.

"You get out of here, you Peeping Tom pricks!" She shrieked, hair wild and eyes doubly so. She made as if to circle around Leech and he stepped between her and the men, not sure who he was protecting from whom.

"Ma'am," one of them began before she let loose a stream of invective that suggested a sailing lineage. They wilted visibly and their flashlights lowered enough that Leech could make out the blunt violence of their features.

"Who the hell are you?" Leech asked.

The men gave each other a look and one said, "Neighborhood wa–" before the woman circled the burning televisions with a jabbing finger and unleashed an entirely new eruption of vitriol, with, as far as he could tell, not one insult repeated from the first salvo.

"I think we're all set here," Leech said, not feeling alright at all but hoping to decrease the number of moving parts in the problem confronting him.

"Ahhh . . . have a good night," one of the watchmen said, and they both walked away in the dark as he turned to face the woman.

Firelight makes anyone beautiful, not that she needed the help. Sweaty and naked, breasts heaving with her panting breath, she was a sight to behold.

He glanced at the melted televisions and hid the knife behind his back. "Ma'am, I need to come clean. I'm sorry about the ruckus, but I'm having a problem." He tapped a finger against his head. "I don't know how much I drank or what pills I took, but I can't remember how this evening started." His throat thickened and sudden tears warmed his eyes. "Christ, I can't remember who I really am."

She stepped across the lawn the way a magic lady

would step from a lake, the kind of woman who might offer swords to heroes. Her hands found his chest, her touch fever hot and her breath sour with booze.

"You're my honeybee," she said, slurring only a bit. "And you're home, baby. You're finally home."

He sunk to his knees as the wind left his sails, the dew soaking through the pajamas. "Do you know my—" His voice hitched. "Do you know my real name?"

She slid to her knees in a way that wasn't entirely graceful, but her fingertips were gentle on his cheek. "Well, your most recent name was Archibald Leech."

"My most recent name?"

"You live a funny life, baby."

2.

He fixed her a martini just the way she liked it and some certainty of self locked into place when he realized he hadn't had to ask. The barrier between this moment and his memory thinning to gossamer. They sat in the dark living room on the floor with their legs crossed, facing each other close enough to pass the cocktail back and forth without spilling.

A funny spray of moonlight crept in through the window to paint her breasts blue and her nipples purple and he shared the observation, which made her laugh, beads of sweat on her skin flashing like sapphires.

"Moonlight sure is funny." He spoke carefully, his mouth rebellious, wondering at his tolerance and the last time he'd had a drink.

"Ain't moonlight, you dummy." She pointed up and leaned over to hand the dregs of the martini to him. "Our little night light."

"You mean they made a moon just for us?"

She nodded, working gin-slicked gears to speak but giddy with more than alcohol. Giddy with him. "Right on the ceiling."

He glanced up at the dimpled landscape of the stucco ceiling but saw no moon.

She shook her head and stood, reaching down to pull him to his feet with a surprising strength. “C’mon.”

Back outside to the dew-dampened grass and the still air and he observed for a second time the muffled quality of the noises around them.

Her fingertips touched the underside of his chin and tilted his head to look up at the sky, with its tiny sparkling stars and round, silvery moon.

“Our nightlight,” she said. “Right up on the ceiling.”

Christ, out there above the house wasn’t a sky at all.

She was right. The house was inside another building, another house maybe, like a Russian doll. He wondered about warehouses and airplane hangars and how a terrarium built for people was a wonderful way to keep hold of a loose cannon such as himself . . . but his awakening self, lubricated by martinis, wondered if this house was the smallest house, or was there another smaller house inside of his? How many houses did it expand out into the universe and was this just a TV show orchestrated by a cosmic director?

(EVERYTHING WENT WHITE)

And then she was guiding him inside and talking low, his wife, his Karen, who took care of him the way he took care of her.

Houses? Who cared? This one had her.

THE FIFTH STORY

1.

LEECH WAS BITING into a tuna melt when the gun touched his ear.

"You're supposed to be in a cell," a deep voice said behind him. "But here you are at the diner."

"I don't know what you're talking about," Leech said around a mouthful.

"Hey folks, now he can speak," the police officer said. Nearby patrons stared, wondering if this would be entertaining or dangerous. "Why don't you tell me your name."

"Archibald Leech."

"Like Cary Grant?" the waitress said from behind the counter.

"Spelled different."

"Flo? We're busy here," the officer said to the waitress. "Stand up and put your hands on the counter."

Leech slid off the revolving stool and placed his palms on either side of his empty plate. The officer groped him as his kind were wont to do and Leech heard, "Hey now!" when the cop fished a Luger from Leech's shoulder holster. The hard metal of a gun barrel pressed against the skin at the back of his neck as nearby customers scattered away from the impending violence.

"Where'd you get this, son?"

"I have a license to carry as a private investigator."

"Not my question." The gun barrel shoved Leech's

head forward and the Panama hat threatened to tumble from his scalp. "You didn't have this an hour ago, so where'd you get it?"

Leech's thin lips pressed together into near invisibility.

The officer leaned in close enough to share the intimate warmth of his breath. "Now that you broke the seal, I'm gonna take you back to the station and you're gonna tell me everything I want to know."

Leech sniffed and decided that as plans went, *stop at the diner before investigating* was not one of his best. Then again, everything about this operation was unusual, even for him.

2.

This is what happened.

Bertha's front tire blew with a bang and the big Lincoln slewed to the right, clipping off a row of corn stalks. She skidded to a stop in a cloud of chaff and for a moment the only sound was the irritated growl of her engine. Then even that was gone.

Leech picked up his fallen cell phone. "Karen, honey?" But the call had cut out and the screen showed no signal. He sent her a quick text about a flat tire, hoping that the message would somehow sneak through even if a call could not.

"Well, dammit."

He pushed open the door and stepped out into the Nebraska afternoon, scanning the uneasy rows of cornstalks crowding either side of the lonely road. Gold filaments of silk floated on the air and he sneezed as the slaughtered corn exacted a petty revenge.

Thoughts of sniper bullets were automatic and he slid a hand inside the breast of his pale linen jacket to unsnap the shoulder holster containing his prized Luger. He distrusted this corn, endless stalks standing in ranks like a Roman legion poised to flood the road with violence.

He distrusted the scarecrows looming above the rustling sea. The figure to his right was about thirty yards from the road, complete with straw hat and lumpy plaid shirt, arms stretched wide to welcome Jesus. The scarecrow to his left was uglier and sagging towards escape, its smashed gourd of a head leaking black. The two guardians were placed so that he couldn't watch both at once and this he distrusted most of all, because he disdained notions of coincidence.

He thought the lack of cell signal was no coincidence either. A toothpick took the place of the cigarette he craved, but he'd promised Karen that he would not call down the cancer and there was no ambiguity about a promise to his wife.

So the toothpick and a grumpy outlook. Archibald the Irritable lost in Nebraska.

"Goddammit." He pushed back his hat and scratched at the sweaty plaster of his hair. Horsetail clouds drifted in the blue sky overhead and a breeze gave the cornfields their voice, whispering secrets about his violent intrusion as leaves rubbed together like the forelegs of a thousand flies.

A black crow said, "What?" from atop a swaying corn stalk and Leech said, "What?" back and he realized it was time for his pills, so he fished two slim plastic bottles from a pocket and swallowed the white tablets, his tongue making smacking sounds because he was dry mouthed without anything to wet his whistle.

"Goddammit."

Nebraska made Arkansas look like New York City.

He cocked his head in the hope of hearing a farmer's combine, though the idea of pushing through the corn to find it held little appeal. He hadn't passed so much as a roadside produce stand in fifty miles and had no idea when this particular road might reach what Nebraskans called civilization. Not that he should put on airs, even an ice box full of Coca-Cola would seem like Shangri-La in the heat.

He leaned inside Bertha and popped the trunk before removing his jacket and laying it across the vinyl of the broad bench seat. Long fingers played the buttons of his sky blue shirt like a piano solo and soon enough, it was stretched atop the jacket along with his shoulder holster. There was brief consideration of removing his pants to avoid the inevitable grease stain, but the thought of being so vulnerable amidst all that hungry corn was too much, and when he balanced the weight of his dignity against the sanctity of his trousers, dignity won.

That it was late September mattered not to Nebraska, a state ornery enough to belong in Appalachia. Nebraska played early fall like it was the height of summer. Leech could taste the salt along his upper lip as he fetched the spare from the trunk with a hoarse grunt. Fair skinned, he felt the prickle of sweat break out across his torso as the sun pressed warm hands against his shoulders. Bertha had been clean before they crossed the border but wore Nebraska like a filthy dress. Dirt around the wheel wells. Bugs in the grill and now a busted tire.

A flash of light shimmered like a heat mirage into the boxy outline of an approaching truck, which he knew for a Ford because of its shape. Without shifting his eyes, Leech reached back into the trunk and flipped the metal catches on a long black case, freeing up the venerable Fabrique Nationale Light Automatic Rifle. The FAL fired a big 7.62 round and felt more comfortable in his hands than a smaller, more modern rifle.

3.

The driver was broad and black with forearms thicker than his own, and after the usual "Looks like you have car trouble" dance, she admitted to having a perfect spare for his Lincoln and hefted it from the back of her tow truck without a grunt.

That she worked for Control was certain. What remained to be discovered was if she was a field operative with unpleasant orders regarding Leech, or today's Face of Control.

As she skillfully worked the lug wrench, she said, "G'wan put your shirt on 'fore you burn."

He did so, slipping on the shoulder holster and jacket while out of her sight line, wondering how many riflemen lurked in the corn or if she intended to use her hands.

"How'd you know to come this way?" Leech asked.

"Didn't." She dumped the shredded tire onto the shoulder in a puff of dust. "You're just on my way."

"Fortunate for me."

"'Spect so." Crows flew up from the corn in an explosion of wings and Leech knew where the sniper waited. He fought the urge to break for the FAL and the driver glanced at him, squinting against the bright sky.

"You ever hear of Gartley?"

"Knew a Shane Gartley," he said. "Fisherman down Pensacola way."

"Not a who, an it," she said with an *aren't you silly* smile. "Town of Gartley 'bout thirty miles north."

Leech looked around at the bland uniformity. "I have no idea which way is north."

The driver looked up as if to say something but shook her head. "You ain't ever heard of it?"

A tic wanted to shiver the corner of Leech's mouth and he forced a smile. "I have not."

A minute later and she was done without the cursing he would have employed. She scribbled on a clipboard and handed it over to him before heading back to the truck. Hefting one buttock onto the seat, she spoke into a CB handset, eyes on him.

He flipped up the invoice and discovered several black and white surveillance photos.

"Who is that?" She leaned out of the truck.

Leech shook his head, speechless.

She dropped the CB handset and lumbered forth from the truck. "Today's your lucky day."

"I'm going to Gartley?"

The woman who was today's Face of Control nodded, beads of sweat like diamonds on her wide forehead. "You're going to Gartley."

4.

Nightfall. Gartley, Nebraska.

Leech was handcuffed and herded from the diner with the officer clutching his triceps. Streetlights were buzzing to life and Leech was treated to the dance of late season fireflies.

It was a place that knew poverty and corn and not much else. The few storefronts were empty, only the diner and a bar open for business.

Leech was shoved across the street towards the only two-story building in sight, where signs reading TOWN COUNCIL and POLICE gave purpose to the structure.

The police station occupied the first floor. Leech said, "Thank you," when the officer opened the door for him. A uniformed cop looked up from the dispatch radio and her eyes grew wide at the sight of Leech. "What the hell?"

Leech was guided past the four desks occupying the main room towards a row of three holding cells in the back, but the officer behind him stopped and said, "What the hell?" Leech glanced at the single, occupied cell and felt his pulse kick.

"What kind of stunt are you pulling?" the officer said, yanking Leech around to face him.

Leech shrugged. "No stunts. I just wanted a tuna melt."

The dispatch officer came up beside them and shook her head, bleached hair permed into a helmet. "Put him in a cell and I'll call the Chief."

"Yeah." The officer who had interrupted Leech's dinner shoved him into the unoccupied middle cell and locked him inside. "No funny stuff."

"Wouldn't think of it," Leech said as the officer retreated. He strolled to the bars separating him from the occupied cell and pushed his hat back to scratch his forehead. The other prisoner slouched on the single cot and met his eyes.

"Hi," Leech said. "I've been looking for you."

5.

Mosquitoes danced in the yellow glare of Bertha's high beams and grasshoppers leapt to their death against his windshield, enough that Leech had to trigger the wipers to clear his view.

The outlying houses were dressed in chipped white paint and sagging porches. More than one sported a squeaking weathervane and dirt driveways displayed an abundance of pickup trucks.

Leaving Bertha concealed on a dirt road that cut through a cornfield, Leech took the heel-toe express towards the center of town. He carried the ID of a private investigator, which gave him an excuse to ask questions but not much in the way of thunder.

Corn grew in yards, along roads and in fields. It looked to Leech as if the crop that had once supported the town was turning the tables to consume the community that planted it. Leech sucked on his toothpick and listened to the whisper of the endless rows and decided he did not like Gartley, Nebraska.

He was passing a roadside billboard that read FIND COMMUNITY IN CHRIST when he realized that he hadn't seen another person since he started walking. No one smoking on their porch or sipping a cold beer. Lights were on inside houses, but the shades were drawn, and he hadn't even heard an engine, let alone seen a car on the road. When he finally did see a silhouette standing behind a screen door, he raised a hand in greeting.

The inside door slammed shut in answer.

"Hey honeybee," he said into his cell phone, in need of words.

But when Karen said, "Where you at?" he knew there was at least one empty bottle in the house and the call would be short.

"Just a funny little town with more corn than people," he said. "You sleep now and I'll call tomorrow."

Lights told him he'd reached the center of Gartley, but even this scrawny place displayed empty sidewalks. Noise leaked from a diner and a nearby bar so he knew that there *were* people in Gartley and he headed that way. A handwritten sign in the plate glass window of the diner boasted BEST TUNA MELT IN GOSPER COUNTY and he decided to put that to the test.

6.

The man had his face.

Not a similar face—*his* face. Leech had a light beard and only needed to shave every other day, but that still amounted to several thousand mornings spent staring at himself in the mirror and he knew that the face the other man wore was his own.

It made him peevish.

"Who are you?" Leech said through the bars. The other man—the other *him*—tipped his head back and dragged a lazy fingertip over the brick wall above his head. He wore a linen suit of similar cut, light like Leech's own, and sported a narrow brim hat identical to the Panama on Leech's head. In the hour Leech had been incarcerated beside him, the other prisoner hadn't spoken a single word.

"Which one of you was eating the tuna melt?"

Leech turned to see a big-bellied, grey-haired man in jeans and a chambray shirt staring at him from the other side of the bars. He wore a gun on his hip and a badge on his chest and he looked almost as baffled as Leech himself.

The chief turned his head back and forth to examine Leech and his fellow prisoner.

Leech raised his hand. "Sign said it was the best in the county."

"Two thousand people in the entire county," the chief said. "The competition ain't stiff." He held up Leech's wallet. "You're Archibald Leech?"

"Yessir."

"Private investigator?"

"Yessir."

The chief turned to the other cell. "Who are you?"

"He ain't said a word since Daryl brought him in," the dispatch officer said.

"Where's your identification?" the chief asked. The prisoner fiddled with a button on his jacket and said nothing. The chief looked at Leech. "You brothers?"

"No."

"Why are you here, Leech?"

Leech tipped his head towards the other cell. "Looking for him."

The chief produced a set of keys and approached the cells. "Want to talk to you in my office. Don't give me any shit."

7.

"This is a small town in a small county in a state with a small population," the chief said, seated behind an old, metal desk. "But I've been a cop for thirty years and in that time, I've learned to distrust coincidences."

The similarity to Leech's own recent thoughts struck him and in that strange way he had, he began to sense the rhythm of unfolding events. He was sitting in a wooden guest chair that squeaked when he moved, and he nodded to encourage the chief.

"We started seeing you," the chief said, "or maybe it was him, about three weeks ago."

"I've never been to Gartley before," Leech said.

The chief waved as if to scatter smoke. "We'll get to that, but since you talk and he don't, I want to see what you think of this coincidence."

"Which is?"

"Corn people."

"Who?"

"That's what townsfolk are calling them. The corn people."

"I don't understand."

"Lot of that going around." The chief opened a box atop the desk and pulled out a cigar without offering one to Leech. He bit off the end and spit it into a wire trashcan before producing flame from a steel lighter with USMC engraved on the side. "About three weeks ago the first person went missing. We figured it was just someone who stayed out drinking and slept in their truck and when they showed up a day later, we didn't think any more about it . . . until it happened again. Then again. Eighteen people have gone missing in the last three weeks, only to wander out of the cornfield within a few days. When they come back, they're different."

"Different how?"

"Dumb, tired, depressed, no memory of why they were in the corn." The chief puffed until the tip of the cigar glowed and the room stank of smoke. "Two weird things happened at the same time. Weird guy spotted around town, doesn't speak or have identification, and then we got people who vanish only to wander out of the corn different than before."

"Weird thing number three." Leech raised three fingers. "He has my face."

"He sure does." The chief gnawed on his cigar and shifted in his seat. "Patrol car picked him up trying to break into a house. Didn't resist or say a word when he was brought in. Your doppelganger hasn't said anything at all." The chief noticed Leech's expression and said, "Yeah, doppelganger. I can even read without moving my lips."

The chief stopped when he heard raised voices outside his office. "Stay here." He jabbed a finger at Leech and raced to the door, hand on the butt of his pistol.

Seconds after he vanished through the door Leech heard a shout and the crash of furniture and sprang out of his chair, intending to charge after the chief—

He froze in the doorway.

The chief and the dispatch officer were sprawled on the floor and a lean man in a linen suit and Panama hat was unlocking the occupied cell. When the prisoner was freed, he stepped up beside his rescuer. The two turned and looked at Leech.

They were identical in every feature and article of clothing . . . and identical to Leech.

The twins glanced at each other and moved to disarm the fallen police officers, tossing the weapons and gun belts aside before gathering up the two cops as if they weighed no more than children.

The body thieves were out the door a moment later.

8.

Night. The cornfield outside Gartley.

The stalks towered over Leech as he followed the body thieves, sometimes racing down a clear path between the rows, sometimes cutting directly through walls of cornstalks.

There wasn't much moon but they made no attempt to conceal their passage and he was able to follow by ear as much as eye, panting and coughing against the dust and chaff as he pushed through the rows, batting aside leaves and cobs and blinking his watery eyes.

Karen liked to yell at TV shows and one of her most frequent refrains was, "Take the gun!" when a celluloid hero felled an armed villain. Leech heard her voice as clear as day in those seconds after his doppelgangers fled the station and having no idea where the officers had stashed his Luger, he helped himself to police weapons. The dispatch officer's gun belt was strapped around his waist and the chief's larger belt was slung across his chest bandito style, brass rounds winking eagerly. Both holsters held .38 revolvers and he hoped they'd be enough for whatever lay ahead.

He tripped over a tangle of fallen cornstalks that had tumbled into a low deadfall. His hat flew off and the chief's revolver slipped from its holster, causing Leech to lose precious seconds crawling on all fours through the corn to retrieve both before he stood.

And noticed silence.

Pulse thundering in his ears, he made an effort to slow his rasping breath and listen for the body thieves, but their crashing passage had stopped. His left hand wiped sweat-sticky cornsilk from his face as his right plucked the .38 from his hip holster.

Are they laying in ambush? Are they circling back towards me?

He sank into a crouch and eased down the row, leaves brushing drily against his shoulders, gun question for a target. He had no qualms about shooting a man who wore his face. Or shooting a pair of them, for that matter.

If he had been moving quickly he would have tripped over the chief. Instead he paused at the shadowy bulk and knelt beside the man, feeling up his body to check the carotid artery for a pulse.

What he discovered were roots.

He fished out his phone and activated the light—

The chief had no face!

Stifling a gasp, Leech leaned closer. A fine network of roots covered the old man's face like a mask, extending like thin fingers into the chief's nostrils and mouth and even his ears.

So close was his study that he didn't notice the legs just beyond the chief and his reaction upon seeing them was to fall back on his seat and aim his pistol at the man in the linen suit and Panama hat . . .

The man whose feet were buried in the dirt.

He was bound to a thick bunch of cornstalks towering behind him, roots circling his torso like so many ropes. His chin was on his chest and the hat concealed his face.

Leech stood, steadying his aim before approaching to lift the concealing hat.

Or tried to. The hat seemed to be attached to the man's head. Leech put more effort into removing the hat and the entire head lifted.

This time, Leech was unable to hold back an explosion of breath as he beheld the eerie countenance. The skin was soft and looked like melted plastic in flesh tones, with the bare hint of features emerging. Shallow caverns for eyes, a smooth bump of a nose.

The unformed man jerked in Leech's grasp and he sprang away, thumbing back the hammer and extending the revolver at the length of his arm. But the thing didn't pull free from its bindings, instead it settled back, knees bending, head slumping forward.

Around him, the corn whispered in approval.

Leech was not above sacrificing strangers in the pursuit of a mission, but this event offended him and he knelt, clawing the roots away from the chief's face, yanking bloody strands from his nose. The faceless man shivered and twitched where it was bound like a witch to a stake but Leech was frenzied in his effort, slapping the chief and whispering encouragement until eyelids fluttered and the old man sucked in a terrified breath.

"What?"

Leech slapped a hand over his mouth but the old man bucked and fought, eyes bulging in terror. Leech straddled him like a schoolyard bully until the chief's struggles weakened. He grabbed the man's clean shaven chin and turned his head to see the unformed homunculus towering over them.

"That corn fella was about to eat you whole," Leech hissed. "You follow my trail back to town and stay out of the rows. You hear me? Stay out of the rows!"

The chief nodded and Leech stood, offering a hand to help the chief to his feet. He yanked the gun belt off his shoulder and held it out. "You go on and let me handle it."

"That thing–" The chief's eyes were locked on the slumped form of the corn man.

"There's things in these rows that you aren't ready to meet," Leech said. "Go. GO!" He shoved the chief and the old man stumbled back before turning and crashing away through the corn with no effort to find the path.

Leech holstered his remaining revolver and removed his hat, sliding nimble fingers beneath the hatband to retrieve the wire garrote concealed beneath it.

The bundle of cornstalks made attacking from behind difficult, so Leech stepped chest to chest with the corn man and looped the garrote around his neck, pulling hard and jamming a knee into a soft belly to increase his leverage.

The effect was immediate as the corn man thrashed against its bindings. Leech redoubled his efforts and a line of fluid oozed from the wound inflicted by the garrote. It lifted its head and stared at Leech with the empty caverns of its eyes as a dimple appeared low on its doughy face. The dimple deepened into a small hole before stretching open, strands of flesh snapping like taffy as it shrieked.

The deadly circle of the garrote closed as the wire sliced completely through the neck. The shrieking ceased as the head tumbled free.

9.

There was light up ahead where the corn thinned. A murmur of voices rose above the whisper of plants. Leech dropped low to crawl, careful about noise. Though he wrestled briefly with the notion of searching for the dispatcher, he proceeded without her. His was a job that often required a stone heart and this night was such a night.

Laughter rang out up ahead. Happy conversation. The smell of grilling meat floated on the night and he clearly heard the word, "Cheeseburger."

It sounded for all the world like a summer picnic.

Lower now, slithering forward until he could peer between stalks like a child peering through his parent's legs.

Two doppelgangers passed mere feet away, holding hands.

"Mom, I'm vegetarian now," the first said.

"Since when?" the second retorted with exasperation.

The argument continued as they walked out of earshot and Leech clearly heard an annoyed, "Lisa," from the doppelganger playing the mother.

In the distance was a three-story house with a wooden sign in front, the windows lit despite the hour. On the wide lawn in between was a cookout. Two doppelgangers played badminton while onlookers shouted insults. Another worked the smoking grill while yet another waited with a paper plate and a hamburger bun.

Different body language. Different speech patterns.

But the same voice. The same face.

His.

Despite the moment, the smell of grilling beef made his stomach gurgle and Leech remembered that he never did get to eat that tuna melt. A hamburger sounded awfully appealing.

10.

He didn't notice the watchers until he was standing third in line behind two doppelgangers talking about tractors, and was embarrassed to admit that imagining the taste of a burger with onions was part of the distraction.

The watchers didn't look any different from the picnickers, but they sure as hell acted differently. They stood still, completely still, half a dozen he could see lined up like sentries around the boarding house. In their stillness he was reminded of the body thieves at the police station, and a theory formed about those townsfolk who returned from the corn as lesser versions of themselves.

The thieves were stealing personalities.

The farmer doppelganger in front of Leech turned toward him. "Who might you be?"

Leech threw his weight on the theory untested. "I've been a cop in this town for thirty years and chief for ten. " Leech laughed. "I think your night vision is startin' to go."

The doppelganger stilled for a moment, eyes unfocused as if processing. That mouth, so identical to Leech's own, split into a smile. "My mind must be going, too, Ray. Don't tell anybody."

"As long as you don't tell anybody I'm eating hamburgers." He patted his belly as if was a fulsome gut, like the chief's. "But I'll be damned if I eat a salad at a cookout."

They laughed and Leech was soon at the grill, saying, "Yes," to cheese and ketchup but, "No," to mustard.

He nodded thanks and took a mouthful to avoid banter with the chef and used the moment to get a closer look at the watchers, who remained as still as statues and seemed unconcerned with Archibald Leech.

A casual scan of the shindig led him to believe there were eighteen picnickers, though certainty eluded him because of their movement and identical nature. The chief had described eighteen corn people, which added a little more weight to the theory. Not to mention that eighteen picnickers added to six watchers meant there were more doppelgangers than he had bullets.

If there were guards around the boarding house, it was reasonable to assume that there was something valuable inside they didn't want him to see. It seemed only responsible to investigate before he called in an air strike and blew the place to hell.

Waving to *Lisa* and her *mother*, he ambled around to the front porch and was pleasantly surprised to see no watchers in sight. The stairs creaked beneath his feet and the Bed and Breakfast sign squeaked overhead. Cursing the lack of a napkin, he licked his fingers clean and pulled open the screen door, wincing when dead bugs fell from the screen.

He was wrong about everything. The boarding house was empty and clean. Even the cellar held nothing more threatening than an excess of spiders.

He was descending the attic stairs when they attacked.

11.

Headlights glared and engines roared. Men shouted—some of them, eerily, with his very own voice. Leech drew his .38 and looked out the window to see a column of farm trucks racing up the driveway while more vehicles approached through the corn, shouldering aside stalks like fire-eyed, prehistoric monsters.

The pop of gunfire was almost an afterthought.

Doppelgangers fell and those he thought of as *picnickers* huddled while headlight beams pinned them in place. It wasn't until he saw six versions of himself racing towards the cornfield with terrible speed that he realized his blunder. They weren't watching the house, they were watching the corn.

He thundered down the stairs and wondered if he'd have to shoot his way through the Gartley townsfolk.

12.

The men of Gartley were furious and frightening but they were no soldiers, and left the half circle of trucks unguarded as they shouted and corralled the doppelgangers in the glare of a dozen headlights.

A plan formed on the fly when he spotted a propane tank in the back of a sturdy Dodge, left with the engine still running. A man in worn overalls and rubber boots saw him and opened his mouth to shout. Leech fed him a mouthful of shooting iron instead and knocked teeth and a cigar flying.

Leech stuck the cigar between his own pearly whites and shoved the gear shift into reverse, backing up with a roar to give himself clearance before gunning the responsive truck across the lawn and straight into the rows.

Blinded and deafened by the rough trip, he had no idea how far he was in and prayed it would be enough, before slipping out of the cab and springing into the truck bed. A match relit the cigar and he cranked open the propane tank until it hissed in warning. The cigar was jammed into the tank's handle and he rabbited.

He ran straight up a row to increase speed as the weakness in the plan revealed itself. *How long would it take for the propane to ignite?* Sooner than he hoped, as it turned out. The world went white and the heel of Jupiter flattened everything.

Leech learned to fly.

13.

Dawn was adding orange to the sky to match the flames below when Leech staggered from the corn. He was soot-faced and his jacket had burned to tatters. Somewhere he lost a shoe.

But the fire was burning wild and whatever was inside the corn was either dead or wishing it was.

Bertha pulled up to the shoulder of the road, making her own clouds of dust. He staggered towards his trusty steed, coughing and nearly passing out. The big tow truck driver emerged from behind the wheel to carry him the last few yards. She threw him in the backseat before spurring Bertha to speed as the first fire trucks began to arrive.

Even in his battered state Leech hated to see someone else driving his car.

When he could speak, Leech briefed her on the clusterfuck of an operation. She spoke into a cell phone, using a code he knew all too well. Control would insert agents among the firemen and make sure that not a single version of Archibald Leech remained in the field.

14.

At a Super 8 Motel—Control was miserly with its per diem—the Face of Control showered and slipped on her favorite kimono to type up her report at the rickety desk. She designated it Corn People, taking the phrase from Leech, and sent it up the chain of command.

Unbeknownst to her, the report caused a stir among the three-piece-suit crowd and it was flagged as an addendum to another report, code name: Brain Colony. This other report, considerably bigger and including video, covered the strange events at an abandoned school campus in 1952. Among the odd details, this bigger report included dossiers of two dozen scientists who had been reported missing.

Among the missing was a man named Archibald Leech.

THE SIXTH STORY

1.

"SPECIAL AGENT LEECH." He held a hand out the car window, flipping open his badge case.

The security guard in the booth nodded and looked at a clipboard. "Visitor parking is over there to the left."

Leech pressed lightly on the gas pedal and Bertha rolled beneath the bland aluminum sign reading BELMONT PSYCHIATRIC HOSPITAL as the electronic gate slid aside. The fence was black iron. Victorian. The grounds maintained as if it were the 19th century. It brought to mind alienists instead of psychologists. Treatment for moral maladies instead of mental illness. The house on the hill was gabled and gothic, overlooking the hospital the way a castle might overlook a village, its tallest level topped with a conical roof almost narrow enough to be a steeple.

Bertha took him along a winding driveway where his eyes were drawn to the massive, stone structure, windows winking in the sunshine. Barred and ancient, it resembled a prison more than a place of healing. His memories of the place were shot through with ruptures. Shaky as if filmed with a handheld camera and then edited to drop in scenes out of sequence.

What he didn't remember was filth. Fast food wrappers scratching across the parking lot as a breeze sent them tumbling. Shards of green glass glinting in the sunlight. Dank brown stains fanning down the walls from drainage gutters at the roofline.

A few people were walking aimlessly on the dead grass of a small park. They wore identical navy coats over hospital gowns. The bare shins on men and women alike were pebbled with gooseflesh. None of them had seen a recent shave.

No hospital staff were in sight.

Leech raised a hand to one woman who stood at the edge of the driveway. She didn't wave back, but watched with unblinking eyes as his car rolled past. He wondered what she was seeing.

Other patients began migrating slowly in his direction as he pulled into the empty visitor's parking lot. So many unblinking eyes tracking his progress. A few attendants emerged from shelter towards the patients. Leech shifted Bertha into Park and turned off the ignition, a sudden billow of smoke blooming around the tailpipe and then vanishing.

A dozen people stood at the edge of the parking lot now, staring. Attendants moved among them and were ignored as Leech climbed from the car and slammed the door shut, the sound too loud in the quiet place. He heard no voices. No traffic on nearby roads. No wind rustled the leafless trees. His heels clocked on the pavement and he wished they were quieter as he walked along a concrete pathway, following signs that read RECEPTION THIS WAY, avoiding pathways that led into the dead park and the staring patients.

A long shadow chilled him and, realizing the sun was already in the west, Leech looked back for the source of solar occlusion.

It was the house, the horrible house, wildly out of step with the 21st century. He blinked to be sure the house was really there, but it stood solid and dark against the sun, despite his effort to banish it. He wondered what the sight did to the damaged minds of the patients and he looked at the blank faces watching him, devoid of any sense. He shivered, realizing that the patients allowed outside were the healthiest and most sound residents of Belmont Psychiatric Hospital.

The real madness was within.

2.

It was a cramped, windowless office colored in dull primer and otherwise unadorned. Leech sat on a metal swivel chair in dire need of oil and placed his Panama hat on the desk. The computer work station was ancient and dusty, possibly powered by steam engine from the chugging heat it emitted as it struggled to open the files Doctor Gupta had given him, he of the shining eyes, their pupils crushed to pinpoints by whatever pills he had eaten.

"It was a massive schizophrenic break and without medication, Ms. Lotz is quite unable to handle normal social interactions," Gupta told him. "You can see her decline in what . . . well, you'll see."

"Whose office is this?" Leech asked.

"Hers." A wide, dry grin below wet, gleaming eyes.

"Wait." Leech held up a hand to stop the doctor from leaving. "That house outside, on the hill. What is it?"

"It was built to house the hospital administrator when the asylum was constructed in 1908. The fire that destroyed the original asylum didn't touch the house and it still serves its purpose, housing Belmont's administrator.

Gupta left after that, humming in counterpoint to the clap of his shoes on the floor.

The file opened onscreen and Leech clicked icons at random, scrolling quickly through poorly scanned newspaper clippings of time travel and alien abductions. Tabloid stuff alongside scholarly articles. He read about table tapping at séances and the CIA's MKUltra experiments during the Cold War. The badly lit screen hurt his eyes and the scrolling made him vaguely queasy.

Leech closed the file and placed a mint toothpick in his mouth while opening another file, lifting his nose and sniffing at the odor of ozone. He drew a circle in the dust on the screen but wasn't motivated to add features and make it a face.

"I'm not sure what help she will be to you," Gupta had said. "But our guests have so few visitors, I'm sure she will appreciate the conversation."

Leech had not shared his previous association with Belmont Psychiatric Facility and had apparently grown healthy enough to be unrecognizable. Or was it simple malaise? Perhaps they knew and didn't care.

More articles crawled beneath the crud coating the screen. Cryogenics. The longevity of people from Okinawa and Sardinia.

A black and white picture of a book appeared. A thick hardcover adorned with the stylized image of a tree. Yggdrasil. The World Tree.

The book was written by Archibald Leech a long time ago.

He plucked the toothpick from his mouth as if afraid he might swallow it.

He had no memory of writing the book.

Closing the file, Leech rubbed a hand over his face, felt the trail of dust it left on his skin. The lights overhead were giving him a headache.

The machine actually vibrated as it struggled with clumsy computer fingers to unfold the next file. A video. Leech placed his palm against the tower and felt heat.

A low res video showed Dr. Gupta sitting at a bland cafeteria table while a woman paced on the opposite side, gown flapping on her thin frame as her hands shook a loose stack of papers in agitation. One of her hands was wrapped in gauze like a club.

He felt his guts twist and bile burned the back of his throat when he recognized the woman as Dr. Lotz.

"Please start again, Dr. Lotz," Dr. Gupta said. "We've got the camera working now."

"John Doe doesn't like cameras for a reason." Lotz stopped and planted her hands on the table, face taut. "You can't put this on YouTube. He'll see."

The doctor waved a hand, palm down. "This is for internal use only, so I can ask colleagues to consult. No one who isn't a healthcare professional will see this."

Lotz's face slid into a baroque mask of gratefulness as she sat down across the table. Leech felt like a voyeur.

"Just tell it the way you want to tell it."

"Can I read to you what I've written?"

"Of course, you've been working so hard on it, I know. There's no right or wrong way to share."

Onscreen Lotz closed her eyes and inhaled. She dipped her head over the pages as if she was preparing to take a bite.

"Hollywood films are shot out of order, their sequence a pure chaos only understood by the director."

She snuck a glance at Gupta, who returned a benign nod.

"An audience member confronted with the raw footage would be confused into incomprehension, lacking the necessary perspective to understand that there is an underlying order to the perceived chaos, an order of budgets and schedules and location availability, all of this happening out of sight of the audience member, without their knowledge, yet vital to the finished film. The audience member is a child unable to comprehend the narrative until the director instructs an editor to reshuffle the scenes into an order he believes the child will understand."

Leech felt a cold sweat break out over his body, a worm of ice water trickling down his spine beneath his clothes. He could see that Dr. Gupta had no idea what Lotz was saying, but Leech knew people who would understand completely. A scientist named Goetz, for one.

He realized he had stopped listening and looked back at the screen. " . . . Lake Vostol."

"What? Damn." Leech grabbed the mouse but the cursor reacted wildly. He couldn't rewind it.

On screen, Lotz trailed off and pushed back her chair with a screech. The doctor said something quiet that might have been, "Stay here with me and read."

"Right." Lotz sat back down and picked up her papers. "The sound. The great booming of the lake striving to get more of itself inside, to fill the honeycomb beneath the turbulent land above. They traversed stone bridges and undulated through tide pools, consuming pale creatures not to feed, no, but to learn, to study with their fearsome intellect. If they could become *other* they could survive the extinction above."

Lotz clawed aside the top page, frantic to continue reading.

"Jesus," Leech said.

"What strange evolution must have taken place in those nacreous spaces?" Video Lotz continued. "Some break in the chain of life had allowed the lowly fungus to dominate, to ascend the food chain. A mycological explosion that both fed and harvested the pallid, slithering things and armored crustaceans alike. Basidiomycota evolved in the blackness, unchallenged and grown huge, aggressive, cannibalistic in a closed ecological system. In Basidiomycota they found their *other*. They consumed it in great quantities and assumed its place in the subterranean food chain of Lake Vostol."

"They learned."

"They became *other*."

"They survived."

Leech rolled his head and his shoulders, uncomfortable as he watched another page floating towards the floor onscreen.

"It was to my incredible horror—" The video stopped

and Leech scrolled the suddenly responsive cursor up to restart it. Saw that he'd watched the entire file.

Wheels squeaked as he slid away from the work station. He straightened his legs and pressed his palms together, fingertips touching his chin as if in prayer.

3.

The bald orderly stopped Leech outside a metal security door. His eyes were red-rimmed and bloodshot, his attitude distant. A tattoo crept from under his collar to across the side of his thick neck. His medical whites were wrinkled. Leech wondered if the man was medicated.

"Do not stop and talk to the patients. If they speak to you, politely disengage and continue moving," the orderly said, twitching in time with a flickering fluorescent light overhead. "Do not give the patients anything, this includes candy you may have on your person, information about yourself, even a pen. Do not give them anything."

The word *patients* dropped like a stone every time it was mentioned. It wasn't a word for humans, it was a word for *things*. The word *guests* was conspicuously absent.

"Do not touch the patients. If a patient touches you, call out and an orderly will remove the patient. Staff is limited beyond this door so please remain calm in the event of an incident."

Leech noticed the peeling paint on the walls and rust on the hinges of the door. He noticed scabs on the knuckles of the orderly's right hand.

"You will now surrender any weapons, sir."

Leech was carrying a Glock to go along with his FBI badge and he slipped the weapon from its holster, popped the clip and glanced in the tube to make sure there was no chambered round. The slide slammed shut with a *clack* and Leech saw a spark of interest in the orderly's blank eyes as he took the gun in one hand and the loaded magazine in the other.

"Please step through the door," the orderly said, nodding at a security camera overhead. A loud buzzer sounded and the lock disengaged.

4.

"Not sure why they sent you in on that side," Jim the orderly said. "Those people are nuts."

Leech followed the narrowly built man into a well-lit hallway. He glanced back at the arena-sized room filled with human automatons. Several stood in a circle staring at the floor while others drifted about the periphery of the room like dust motes.

"Good you didn't disturb them," Jim said. "Best for everyone when they stay quiet."

"What were they looking at?" Leech stepped up beside the smaller man to match his pace.

Jim shrugged. "Who knows? They're crazy. You get used to just accepting that around here. Frankly, I don't want to see what they're seeing. I think you have to be completely off your rocker to do that, know what I mean?" The orderly's eyes twinkled.

"Jesus." Leech thought about where he went when the Activator hit his veins.

"Yeah, we got some of that here, too," Jim said. "What we don't have is adequate staff or budget. Hey, you don't have a cigarette, do you?

Leech shook his head. "Sorry, no."

Jim shrugged. "It's like nobody out there smokes anymore, but there's nothing else to do in this darn place. C'mon."

Jim nodded forward and led Leech up the hall.

"You get lost again, Mr. Leech, you just follow the blue line on the floor," Jim said, his tone more tour guide than asylum orderly. "Not the yellow, the blue one. Patients here haven't figured out that system yet." He shook his head sadly.

They passed a few rooms where patients lay on cots reading, or sat at desks drawing. Leech's discomfort grew.

"Yeah, it'll be good for Lotz to see you. She doesn't have many visitors. *Any* visitors. And we've all heard her stories too much to listen any more." Jim picked at his teeth with a fingernail. "Crazy shit. Give you nightmares. Did you know she used to be a doctor right here?"

Jim stopped outside a door and pressed a hand against Leech's chest, halting him.

"Okay now, if Lotz gets feisty, you step on out and follow the blue line."

Leech glanced at the floor and offered a nod.

"Sure you ain't got any cigarettes?" Jim said.

"None," Leech said.

"Well, anyway, it'll be good for Lotz to see you. Real good."

5.

"I ate my fingers because I was terribly hungry, not to plant in the ground. I understand that now."

Lotz pulled her left hand from the blanket at her waist and fluttered it in the air gaily. The pinky and ring fingers ended in stumps of shiny scar tissue.

"It was sickness, you see. A hallucinatory break from reality that allowed me to shield a portion of my psyche from the physical damage to my brain. The coma lasted a week, but I was floating untethered to my corporeal self for years. Entering and re-entering a time stream, like jumping ahead by chapters in a movie. I was terrified to the point that some inner circuit breaker switched over and created a fiction."

Lotz smiled calmly as she slid her maimed hand back

under the edge of the blanket. There was a slight dent in the curve of her forehead that he didn't remember from his days as a patient.

Her plastic chair was pressed firmly against the wall.

"The things I saw," she whispered.

Leech gave her a moment to return to herself. "Do you know who I am?"

"I've always known."

"Did you know when you were my doctor?"

"You ask questions as if the scenes go in order, one moment progressing to the next."

"Maybe that's how I perceive them."

"Is it?"

He thought about the Activator slamming into his bloodstream, lighting his circulatory system on fire. He thought about scales sliding from his eyes. "I don't know."

"You know, I don't remember most of our time together. I don't remember anything after we visited that cemetery . . . " She smiled and he remembered the kindness of her voice when he was lost in the sea of his consciousness, an ocean without shores that bled into others until the notion of self stretched into transparency. "But I'm glad you grew healthy enough for release."

He opened his mouth to say something. To apologize for the men who ran them off the road and snatched him away. But maybe it was better that she didn't remember that violent moment.

"It's okay," she said. "It can be hard to hold clear thoughts in this place." Her hands fluttered as if to trace shapes in the air. "This level of existence," she pinched her own arm, "isn't meant to perceive anything beyond the intended order. We don't," she tapped her temple, "have the right equipment. It's like filtering a megawatt laser through eyeglass lenses. Blow them right out of the frame."

Her hands were still talking and he wondered what they were saying.

Leech sat on the opposite side of the white room with his pocket notebook resting on his thigh, his Panama hat resting on the other knee. Illumination poured in from a glass skylight far overhead and reflected from the mirror in the hall to shine into the room. Lotz noticed Leech's gaze.

"To keep the shadows out," Lotz said. "Lighting is very important and shadows are sneaky things." She gestured overhead at empty light fixtures. "When they first gave me a room, I tore out all the lights. This room is a very big help, since I can't turn off the lights no matter how manic I become."

"My hallucination boasted titans of blazing radiance, of great lights that struck with such force they pinned me to the earth like a butterfly in a book." She tapped her temple again. "My machinery was not able to process what I was experiencing." She leaned closer and he mirrored her. "How would our visual sense cope with a ten-dimensional experience? Much like a snippet of film trapped in the projector, it would blaze brightly before shimmering to ash."

A wink.

"The good doctors have ensured that I have light so that my psyche won't, how did they say it . . . *seek the path of least resistance and return to that dark place.*"

Leech's seat was made of clear plastic, devoid of dust or spots of any kind.

"Madness, sadly, is not stupidity. In my case, I was easily able to make shelters out of bedding. Window curtains. What have you. This blanket," she said, lifting the blanket so Leech could see the loose weave, "lets the light shine right through, which is good. It's very good."

Lotz smiled politely from her own seat, identical to Leech's. A spray bottle of Windex sat on the floor beside her chair, along with a roll of paper towels. A transparent plastic waste basket helped keep even small shadows at bay.

"Do you find it too bright? I'm now quite accustomed to it, but it was disconcerting at first."

"I'm alright, Dr. Lotz. Thank you."

"It's alright." She shrugged. "Standards have slipped of late at Belmont and I suspect we could lower the light if we wanted. They don't check on us so often anymore . . . "

"What is it?"

She shrugged again. "It's hard to take myself seriously, but things have really changed around here." She winked. "People are acting funny."

"Funny how?"

"Even here there are norms. Most of the staff has left. Or they don't come in. Dr. Matthews no longer comes down from his house to visit the hospital. A number of the patients . . . " She tilted her head. "There was a time when my peers considered me a good doctor. I can recognize the effects of new medication. Untreated illness. But they're not acting like that."

"The patients."

"The patients, yes."

"What are they acting like?"

"Like they're not the patients."

Leech opened his mouth and closed it without speaking.

"There but for the grace of God go I?" Lotz said.

"Something like that," Leech said.

Lotz chuckled. "It's perfectly understandable. Insanity can be unsettling." She gave Leech a frank look. "Oh I know it's not politically correct to use that word, but let's call it what it is."

Lotz smiled at Leech's wince.

"I explain all this as a demonstration of why I cannot possibly help you. You arrived as John Doe and we saw the grave of Archibald Leech, who was born before you and I took our first breath. Whatever else I *knooooow* . . . ." The word dragged out until Lotz returned to the moment.

"Among the Titans you strove, all colors and no colors but in some sense a chromata I could cling to. We all did. Experiencing the Titans broke my mind and permanently altered this place, this hospital. I wonder what happened to the Titans when they experienced *you*?"

She laughed and gestured overhead.

"Under this bright sunlight, my talk of Titans sounds even more absurd, yes?"

"I don't think anything you've said sounds absurd," Leech said. "And any information you have at all is of use."

Lotz tilted her head, giving Leech a sly glance. "Perhaps this will be of some help?"

She rose and crossed to a stack of books in the corner, lifting what looked like a small photo album off the floor.

"There is almost nothing online about Lake Vostol beyond the most basic information. I began with your book—the book written by the Archibald Leech who died in 1952—and had a difficult time digging deeper. My doctors allow me to look into it as a part of my therapy. But there are other pieces of information, losses during the Soviet dig. Aircraft. Vanished herds."

Lotz closed the book with a snap and held it out, business-like. Leech crossed to her and took it, but Lotz didn't release her grip. His gaze lingered on the stumps of her fingers where they pressed against the cover.

"They give us safety scissors in the common room during crafts period—under close supervision, of course," Lotz said. "The orderlies delight in giving me the scissors with the green rubber handles. Lefty scissors."

"I understand," Leech said.

Leech met Lotz's gaze and tension seeped from Lotz. Her shoulders lowered noticeably.

"You do, don't you?" Lotz said, quietly surprised. She studied the scarring on Leech's face. "Yes?"

"It's as if the entire world tilted over by a single

degree," Leech said. "Just enough that things have slid ever so slightly from where they were."

She stepped closer and dropped her voice. "Do you believe a woman should be allowed to maintain at least a few fictions, Mr. Leech?"

"I'd wake up screaming every morning without them."

Lotz released her hold on the book and Leech tucked it under his arm. "Thank you for speaking to me like an adult." Lotz extended her right hand. "Sometimes I forget what it's like."

They shook hands and he slipped his pocket notebook back inside his coat. He hadn't written down a single thing.

"Dr. Lotz?" Leech paused in the doorway. "Is there anything I can do for you?"

Lotz smiled as she returned to her chair. "I don't think so, Mr. Leech," she trailed off and cocked her head to one side, then rested her gaze on the visitor. "If you were ever inclined to visit again, I would be curious to hear about what you learn."

"Learn?"

"About Titans and gravestones and men." She lowered her gaze. "I'll understand if you don't want to come back here."

Leech nodded. "I don't, to be completely honest. But I don't think one more visit will kill me."

"When I was a girl, my father would wake me up and say, early bird gets the worm. When I got home from school he'd say, what's the story, morning glory?" She nodded at him. "What's the story, morning glory?"

"I have no idea."

"But you'll tell me when you find out?"

"Yes."

Her gratitude was dignified but apparent.

"I shall look forward to it," Lotz said. "Bonne chance."

"Good luck to you, too."

6.

The grounds were clear of the shambling, vacant-eyed husks he'd encountered on his arrival, and Leech held Lotz's album open to read as he walked, trusting his peripheral vision to avoid tripping over the curb.

His pulse picked up as he read. Lotz was a skilled researcher, broken mind or not, and had connected a series of dots that had struck Leech as random islands of information. Much in the way an astronomer looked at the sky and saw bears and gods and monsters, when Leech only saw points of light.

The wind fluttered his linen jacket and plucked at the pages, flipping them to a laminated map of New Hampshire, annotated in different colored markers. Was this the campus that Archibald Leech (in his mind he could share a name with the man) had been driven to in a cherry Packard while the Korean War raged and the Super Powers split the atom with ever-increasing aggression?

Asphalt rippled in the fading light. Was it time for his medication? Or was the fabric of Belmont so laced with psychosis that he had dragged a cloud of madness along with him when he departed?

His phone thrummed with the theme music from *Jaws* and he stopped in the middle of the parking lot, unable to walk, read, and answer the phone simultaneously.

"Leech," he said without looking. He had assigned the ominous stringed instruments of *Jaws* to calls from Control.

Small hairs rose on the back of his neck and he stiffened, glancing around to ensure no one was close. The lot was empty save for old Bertha. The voice continued speaking, using a simple voice changer to render the caller unrecognizable.

A moment later the call concluded. The sun was setting. It would be dark soon.

THE SEVENTH STORY

1.

OF COURSE IT began in a graveyard.

Of course it began at night.

Archibald Leech edged reluctantly among granite markers. He was ill-equipped for the mission, assigned in haste while reporting at Control HQ. Lacking even a flashlight, he worked by the shine of the full moon, armed with little more than his favorite Luger and the aging black Lincoln, Bertha. Her store of Activator had not been reloaded for the mission and he was having trouble remembering his medication. A mission born in haste and all that.

The October wind whistled through the valley and pried at his scarf with icy fingers, attempting to lift his Panama hat. Damn him for jetting off without even a basic kit. The linen suit, while fashionable, was no match for the cooling Fall air and the scarf was a thin thing with Colonial Williamsburg written along it in 18th Century script. It was a gift he had picked up for Karen, commandeered for the job.

Was it a coincidence that his very own grave resided within the cemetery? Of course not, Control had to know. They must've known that this particular boneyard was only an afternoon's drive away from the asylum from which they had plucked him, broken in mind and body after a confrontation in the place beyond reality that scientists called Backstage.

Did they know? He had never spoken of his madman's incarceration to anyone, not even Karen, and he had no reason to believe Dr. Lotz would have spoken after agents from Control ran them off the road and snatched Leech from her broken vehicle.

Insanity. He recalled Dr. Lotz, herself damaged beyond repair, discussing the difficulty a sane person had standing next to the insane. Insanity. Was the Clozapine circulating through his blood stream? Was Risperidone wrapping chains around his unstable id? Or was he about to emerge without the benefit of Activator? Archibald Leech, madman.

Why did Control send him out like this?

Pulling his linen jacket tight against himself, he stepped out of the windy gust into the lee of a decrepit mausoleum. Faces were carved into the stone. Surprisingly lifelike yet utterly devoid of expression, as if the stone were elastic and the faces were pressing through from inside the mausoleum . . . Leech stepped away, shaking off the image. It was a trick of the eye, nothing more.

Too soon, he found it.

The hole had a blasted look, like a violent wound in the hard ground. Runnels of dirt were flung nearly a dozen feet and the pauper's headstone had toppled into the hole, cracking in pieces.

Placing his Panama hat on the grass, he slid down into the grave in a cascade of dirt and pebbles. At the bottom he knelt and lifted a heavy stone piece of the marker. The moon was bright enough that with a little squinting and guesswork, he could make out a date carved into the stone. 1952. Tiny hairs stood up on the back of his neck and he shivered from more than cold.

He popped his head up like a prairie dog from a hole and scanned as much as he could see of the graveyard, ensuring that he was nowhere near the grave bearing the name Archibald Leech.

Moon shadows gave movement to the humps and stones in the cemetery, but he could make out enough to know he was not near that other grave.

1952. The same year the other Archibald Leech was buried.

There were no coincidences.

He shifted position in the tight confines of the hole and his shoulders dislodged more dirt, which tumbled inside his collar and made him shiver. He forced his fingers in between the rigid grit and the stone and lifted another chunk of the marker, but the moonlight was too weak for him to discern the spidery scrawl. Reaching into a side pocket, he withdrew a matchbook and struck a Lucifer alight. Flickering yellow illumination crawled across the pitted stone and revealed an epitaph. LIVE FAST, DIE YOUNG AND LEAVE A BEAUTIFUL CORPSE.

That was nothing he or that other Archibald Leech would ever say. He shook out the match and let the stone fall, leaning back in relief as fingers tickled his neck.

He yelped and whirled, tripping over the gravestone, bouncing against the walls of the pit. He clawed against the dirt, fingernails peeling back as he held himself upright and finally managed to turn completely.

It was just a root exposed long ago by gravediggers and now dangling from the earthen wall of the grave.

He smeared dirt across his brow when he tried to arm away the clammy sweat, cradling his fingers until the sharp pain in their tips subsided. Goddammit, he needed that Activator. He needed his Risperidone and worried about maintaining an even keel without it. A crazy Leech was a bad Leech was a dangerous Leech and he—

A sudden punch against the chunk of headstone sent shockwaves of pain through his knuckle and into his wrist, bringing him back to the moment.

He was ready to work.

Climbing from the hole, he crawled across the

crackling grass until he found a pair of dents in the turf that reminded him of knees. Following on his own hands and knees, he saw a piece of turf torn aside by what he assumed was the heel of a shoe. Several chunks of earth led off to the east.

Leech stood and crumpled a dry clump in his hand, letting it trickle between his fingers. East. Belmont Psychiatric Hospital was to the east.

There were no coincidences.

Climbing atop a thick monument, he balanced precariously, a living gargoyle looking to the east for movement, for the silhouette of a man.

He saw the lights of a distant house.

2.

After scaling the graveyard fence, a half hour of cross country hiking over hill and dale brought him to a small, Cape Cod style dwelling. From the outside all looked well. A single car parked in the driveway. A Halloween pumpkin, as yet uncarved, sat on the step.

Inside, the place was a charnel house.

Crusted smears of blood streaked the walls. Lamps were smashed. Tables and chairs were overturned. A man was scattered across the room in several pieces, torn limb from limb. Somewhere a phone was off the hook and the incessant beep-beep-beep clawed at his self-control.

He focused his vision on a single, bloody handprint on the wall. Never mind that the severed hand that made it was lying against the baseboard.

Nothing lived in the house.

More importantly, nothing moved.

He holstered the Luger and followed telephone noises until he located the phone and returned it to the cradle.

On the rug beside the phone an old phone book was spread open, pages torn from it.

So, the revenant could read.

Why did the revenant stop at the house to kill? Was it simply to check an address? Was it mad and thirsting for blood? Spying a tall glass case in the corner of the living room, Leech broke the glass with an elbow and reached inside to unfasten the door.

Inside the gun case was a pair of elegant, double-barreled shotguns of an old make. Retrieving one, he saw the date 1912 burned into a wooden stock and broke the weapon open to sight down the tubes, inhaling the scent of gun oil. A small drawer on the gun case revealed a box of shells, gauge of twelve. Two shells were fed into the weapon and a handful went into his right front pocket.

An old weapon for an old corpse.

So armed, Archibald Leech made the long march back to where Bertha waited outside the cemetery. If he was right, he knew where the thing was going and Bertha would get him there ahead of time.

If he was right.

"No coincidences."

He rolled the dice.

3.

Black night. The house was high-peaked and looming, surrounded by a wrought iron fence as spidery thin as an ink drawing. It was a gothic sculpture crouched on a bluff, connected to the asylum below by a winding road.

The Administrator resided within. Lord of Belmont Psychiatric Hospital.

Dr. Matthews, who never visited the hospital below.

Leech should have known it would play a part in his story. Both time and reality were fictions designed to protect the fragile mind, tissue-thin barriers between vulnerable grey matter and the Deep. When the house eagerly signaled to him in the period of his incarceration and later in the time of Dr. Lotz's madness, he should have known.

"You are an ugly bastard of a place." The words hissed over thin lips as he sat in his car and let the cooling engine tick while he stared up at the grim cliché. Window shutters banged in the wind. That didn't help.

Spread out below was the fortress-like psychiatric hospital, lights blazing along the fence line. The parking lot was empty and he saw no sign of movement. With the gate closed, he surmised that the revenant would be exposed if it attempted to climb the chain link fence.

He pushed open the door and unfolded from Bertha's embrace before shoving the door closed, wincing at the loud bang it made.

Tick . . . tick . . . tick . . . the engine. His heart. The clock counting down the minutes for the revenant's next victim.

The moon was hidden behind clouds. No streetlights lined the road. An ozone smell tickled his nostrils.

He stepped forward but stopped when he realized that the clacking of a swinging window shutter was matching his footsteps. He shoved his hands deep into his coat pockets and stepped forward again.

The gate squealed in oxidized protest as he pulled it open.

Oh hell yes, the place was calling to him like an eager child.

He stepped through into the yard and sensed a pressure building around him. The shutter was banging more quickly now, clack-clack-clack. He fought to keep his breath slow but it wanted to be quick and shallow, air barely pulling into the top of his lungs before it rushed out again.

If a house could cast a shadow in the dark, then he stood in it.

The explosion dumped quarts of adrenaline into his bloodstream, the animal portion of his brain screaming *flee*

flee even as the more encyclopedic section of his mind noted the crash of thunder.

Rain came down with a whoosh. Stinging pellets of water struck his exposed face and hands. He hunched in his thin jacket and laughed, the adrenaline strangling his mirth into a breathy cackle. The cliché was complete. His next laugh came easier and was more genuine.

He hurried to the front step and . . .

The door was open.

Leech froze, oblivious to the rain pelting him, his eyes unable to discern anything in the pitch-blackness of the foyer. Then he was turning and running across the squishy wet ground until he banged against the fence. He wrenched open the gate and slipped, sprawling into the runoff beside the road and soaking his knees. He imagined the black maw of the open door leering at him, poised to vomit forth an unspeakable horror.

Then he was up and at the trunk of his car, fumbling out his keys, missing the lock on the first try.

The doorway was still dark and empty.

He opened the trunk and the wind fought him, driving the rain sideways against his face and neck.

He lifted out a long leather satchel. Tearing the zipper in his haste, he yanked out the gleaming black length of the 1912 shotgun. He broke the weapon open and checked the two heavy shells, patting the bulge of additional shells in his pocket.

Cradling the weapon at port arms, he stalked the open doorway of the house as if it were a crouching animal ready to spring. He couldn't see more than a foot into the darkness within.

The hammers clicked when he thumbed them back.

In a flapping mass of jacket and limbs he charged through the door and into the foyer. He sensed the inner wall at the last moment and spun, slamming his back into it. His gun, eyes, ears and *feeling* stabbed at the stygian black but found nothing.

A simultaneous flash-boom of lightning and thunder strobe-lit the foyer, deafening him. The after image danced in his eyes. Two doors and a wide staircase going up.

Pulse pounding in his ears he tried to reach out and sense the presence he sought, but fear blocked him. Would it be the attic or the cellar? It was always the attic or the cellar.

The house laughed.

He checked the bottom floor first, edging into rooms, waiting for lightning flares through the windows to flash-paint the picture for him. The place was oddly bereft of furniture save for the occasional ancient overstuffed chair or carved table. Here and there new appliances contrasted sharply. A microwave. A television. As if the house were caught in a shift between the ages, between Victorian and modern.

When he realized the house had no cellar he almost gave a giddy laugh. Almost.

Lightning. Pause. Thunder . . . the eye of the storm was moving farther away.

Too soon Leech found himself at the base of the staircase, curving wide above him. His eyes were adjusted now, their pupils black and engorged to gobble every scrap of available light. But the floor above was dark and impenetrable to his vision.

He couldn't ascend those stairs blind. The first floor of the house had sucked dry his courage.

He retreated to the dining room where a silver candelabra rested atop the elegant table.

Flash . . . boom. Light washed through the windows.

He lit the five candles and felt something within him loosen as the warm yellow glow flickered. The candles quietly hissed and popped, as if burning rendered fat instead of wax.

Holding the candelabra before him like a talisman, Archibald Leech ascended the staircase.

Again the search, room by room

Nothing lurked in the bathroom.

He set the candelabra on the floor and tugged open a closet door with a startling screech. Dirty linens were the only threat. He moved on.

No corpses or bloodstains marred the well-appointed master bedroom with its enormous four poster bed and oak dressers.

Re-entering the hall, Leech crowded behind the candelabra as if its circle of light might dart off and leave him behind. Having the light was almost worse than not having it. His pupils had shrunk down to nothing again. He couldn't see anything beyond the sphere of radiance before him and felt the continuous need to whirl about and bring the light to bear behind him. Clammy sweat mingled with the cold rain soaking his clothes. He sniffled repeatedly.

The storm outside grew feeble and the rain trickled away.

The next room was a child's bedroom. It startled him with its contrast to the rest of the dwelling, his wavering candlelight dancing over a ruffled girl's bedspread and a litter of stuffed animals. A rugged Fisher-Price record player stood proudly amidst a scattering of hand-me-down 45s. The bed was rumpled.

When he emerged again into the hall he heard it . . . a slow, thick dripping.

He followed the sound to the end of the hall. Dark liquid oozed from the cracks around a trap door set in the ceiling.

The attic.

Letting the long-barreled shotgun point off target, he stretched onto his toes, snatching at the cord and yanking sharply—

A weight struck his face and a cascade of warm liquid splashed down across him. His shotgun BOOMED massively and plaster exploded from the wall as he was knocked off his feet.

The candles were snuffed out and pitch black smothered the hall.

The undertaker crabbed backwards as he heard a moaning from overhead, "Maaaaa . . . .maaa . . . maaa," and a scuttling sound in the hall itself.

He levered himself into a sitting position as his thumb flew over the hammers of the shotgun—only one barrel had fired. He threw the weapon to his shoulder, aimed blind and clutched the trigger.

Two feet of flame belched forth from the weapon as the deer slug flung itself lethally at a spot four feet in the air . . . an empty spot.

The undertaker held his breath, trying to sort the split-second image from the muzzle flash. The spattering rain of blood from the attic and beneath it the huddled form of a child.

He strained to listen . . . strained to feel . . . but his fear still crushed that delicate sense.

"Maaa . . . maaa . . . maaa . . . " still echoed hauntingly down from the attic. In front of him, in the hallway, he heard tiny whimpering.

He dropped the first match from trembling fingers but managed to light the second.

Stepping forward behind its weak glow, he beheld a small girl shaking with terror. She was drenched red-black in blood and her eyes were huge white saucers.

"Child?" he croaked through a strangled throat, dizzy from adrenaline. She made no response.

He found the bloody candelabra and plucked a candle from it, then broke open his shotgun to extract the two spent shells, shuddering at how close he had come to blasting the little girl.

With two new shells loaded, he closed the shotgun. "I'll be right back." He unfolded and followed the feeble glow of his candle as he climbed.

"Moaaaaaaooooo . . . " moaned the thing in the corner. The wife. Her mouth worked but language eluded her.

"You're safe now," he whispered, but the woman was oblivious to his presence. Her eyes were fixed on something else.

Horror.

Dr. Matthews had been strung to an overhead beam by his feet, directly over the trap door. The girl must have been huddled beneath her father when the undertaker had pulled the door open.

The dangling man was savagely eviscerated, completely drained of his organs and fluid. The hatred that had fueled the act was a musky stink befouling the air.

4.

Unmanned by his illness and lack of medication, Leech knew he was out of his depth. Whatever the revenant was plotting was beyond him. He imagined the Face of Control growling, "Do your job." Control who had sent him out against a thing that crawled from the grave. Sent him against the thing without his hotshot of Activator.

"You sonofabitch."

His cell phone crackled with interference but he found a working phone in the foyer downstairs, an old device that had held pride of place on the same narrow table for decades.

His finger worked the rotary dial.

"Baby?"

He heard a cough from the other end and a pre-linguistic sound that suggested hours of drinking.

"Karen, it's me. I need your help."

"Help?" He could hear her trying to focus and loved her for it. "You s'possed to be callin' me? Ain't you on a job?"

"They didn't give me—I don't have my meds and my thinking is all muddy, honeybee."

Fury made the line crackle with static as she said, "They what?"

"There's a thing walkin' the earth that shouldn't be walkin' at all," he said, imagining the listeners on the line. "Way I am now, this thing is beyond me." He mopped his damp brow, hand shaking where it held the receiver. "I can't follow through."

"Then you run." A flat snarl. Love and fury burning right through that cheapshit Russian vodka she drank. "You run straight home to me."

"I can't do that." He felt beads of sweat popping out all over his skin. Withdrawal. This was deep shit for sure. "Lady who helped me, a doctor lady, she's right on the tracks and this thing is a runaway train. I don't know what to do, honeybee." He sounded maudlin and didn't care. "I can't finish the job and don't feel right about running."

"Breathe, baby," she commanded. "You breathe and you listen, you got one job. You only got one job. Come home to me, you hear? You come home to me."

"But—"

"But me no buts, mister," she interrupted. "You listen to my voice, you anchor that wonderful, special mind of yours to me, you hear?"

And he did. He listened to his Karen. His rock.

"You go get that doctor lady who helped you and spirit her right out of there. Anything gets in your way you cut it down, you hear?"

He coughed as his throat seemed to thicken, choking his air.

"I said, *you hear*?"

"I hear."

"You hear what?"

"Save the doctor lady. Cut it down if it gets in my way."

"What's your one job?"

"Come home to you."

"That's right, goddammit." Her crying awakened

something in his guts. Something that coiled, alive and mean. "You have to come home to me!"

His molars ground together so hard they creaked. Upstairs he heard the wails of a heartbroken family even as his wife sobbed on the phone.

His own eyes dried as chemicals danced in his brain and he smiled his bar-clearing smile. A unique excretion slithered into his bloodstream and he could feel it.

Maybe his very own Activator.

"Be right back, honeybee," he said. "Got to see about a thing."

5.

False dawn.

Running.

A pile of red and yellow leaves lined the grass along the fence. Cornstalks were tied around the light post at the corner and a sheet-turned-ghost hung with macabre Halloween glee from a tree branch. The most out of place decorations in the world.

Leech kicked leaves every which way as he hit the black iron bars at speed. Luger back in the holster and the shotgun shifting from hand to hand, he scrambled up and over, as noisy as a marching band with cymbals.

The smart move was to circle the facility and look for a back way in, but Leech felt the press of time and sprinted flat out across the empty parking lot, his scarecrow shadow dancing wildly in the yellow glare of the sodium lights.

Something rustled in the bushes alongside the hospital proper. Unaware of the lurking horror, lights blazed inside the facility and through the glass front doors.

A dark shadow lurched onto the concrete walk leading to the main entrance.

Leech skidded to a stop like a runner sliding into second base. He threw the shotgun to his shoulder and took aim.

BOOM.

Four feet of flame lanced out across the distance and the shadowy shape was slammed forward against the glass doors hard enough to shatter them.

Leech broke the shotgun and plucked the smoking shells free, scrabbling two more from his pocket to reload.

Screams rang out inside the foyer as Leech trotted forward with the long gun at port arms. A chair bounced out onto the walk and he kicked it aside as he closed on the chaotic scene.

The revenant was up on its feet, a dirt-encrusted man in a filthy suit. He turned and threw a security guard outside after the chair. Several patients watched the struggle, as unmoving as statues.

The revenant saw Leech.

"Stop!" Oh, that was good.

The revenant stepped into the glow from the lights over the main entrance and Leech fought down nausea. Dirt and leaves clung to the creature from its violent, cross-country journey. A sharp stick jutted from its collarbone, piercing flesh, unnoticed. His suit was tattered and crusted with dried blood from the recent kills. Decay sank its destructive claws into the revenant's gray flesh. His eyes had drained and fallen back into the sockets like the skins of empty grapes.

But the mushrooms were the worst. Toadstools and fungal growths covered every inch of exposed skin. The ragged hole in his chest leaked fibrous white stuff that stank of rancid cottage cheese and looked worse. A hole through which light leaked . . .

And didn't seem to bother the revenant at all.

"Hey, daddy-o," he murmured, a clump of moss tumbling from his mouth, its tongue slathered with a growth of pale enoki mushrooms that shivered on their stems.

The thing stepped forward and Leech backpedaled,

drawing the Luger and flicking off the safety with a practiced movement.

"Don't you remember me, Archie?"

Comprehension came to him on a delay as his mind untangled the mush of words. Shock hit his bloodstream as he heard his own name and his finger crushed the trigger. The Luger snapped in his hand and he kept firing, fifteen rounds that drove the thing staggering back as grave dirt and white slime were flung from its torso.

The last round was carefully aimed, Leech sliding his right foot sideways and extending his arm full length in the manner of a duelist.

The revenant's skull jerked back as a round took it in the eye and he sat down hard, an ear or mushroom tumbling from its head to bounce on the ground.

The thing stood without so much as a grunt of effort, a stringy, curd-like substance leaking from its eye and dangling from the exit wound on its temple.

"Archie!" He grinned hideously, arms thrown wide. "It's all for you—"

Leech twisted at the hips and flung the shotgun sidearm. The whirling length of wood and steel struck him in the shins and the revenant toppled forward. Leech was running before he hit the ground, stuttering left around the thing as the revenant thrashed up. Fingers snatched at the hem of Leech's jacket and fabric ripped, but Leech was already in the lobby and sprinting past the unmoving patients, who followed him with their eyes.

He blew the lock off the first set of doors as an alarm bell clanged.

6.

Dr. Lotz stood in the center of her bright room with her head held high, awaiting whatever might come through the door. The ringing alarm wasn't enough to drown out the sound of distant screams.

When Archibald Leech skidded through with a gun in each hand and red blood splashed across his white linen suit, he had the Devil in his eyes.

She picked up a canvas bag full of her things.

"What's the story, morning glory?"

7.

"Why are you helping me?"

"My wife told me to."

"Why did she tell you to help me?"

"Because you helped me when I was lost. She'd turn the world upside down to help you."

"How could she do that?"

"Set me loose."

8.

"I'm not taking you to Maine," the cab driver said, leaning against his green Owner Operated Taxi as he smoked a cigarette. A cold wind whistled across the crowded parking lot, rustling a blanket of dead leaves, and Dr. Lotz pulled the hood of her Georgetown sweatshirt over her stubbled scalp.

"Boston," Archibald Leech countered, scanning the parking lot. Dr. Lotz shivered by his side, lost within a baggy sweatsuit in the grey and blue of Georgetown University. Her eyes were hollow and she had developed a tic at the left side of her mouth as the meds wore off. She had held up well during the train ride from DC but Leech had no idea how much farther she could make it.

"For a thousand bucks? Four hours on the road with no return fare?"

Control had police waiting at the platform, but the

attempt to corral passengers was disorganized. Leech led Dr. Lotz straight outside where he suggested they skip the taxi line—which was monitored by an officer wearing ear muffs—and found the green taxi with its light off in the lot amidst the minivans and SUVs.

"That's more than you'll make the rest of your shift." Leech expected that the sight of cash in his hand would move the driver to action, but the coarsely whiskered man in the stained green jacket was jaded by life and incapable of excitement.

"You part of this stuff?" The cabby tilted his unshaven chin at the station. "I mean, you two are on the run, right?" His smile was uglier than his resting expression. His were teeth best kept hidden.

"My husband." Dr. Lotz offered a strained smile. "We just need some distance so he can calm down." She tugged the sweatshirt's hood up over her stubbled scalp but there was no hiding that she was ill.

"That so?"

"Yup."

One salt and pepper eyebrow rose over a red-veined eye and the cabby pushed up a Ravens cap to scratch his head. "Fifteen hunnert and I'll take you to New Haven."

"What—" Leech started but Dr. Lotz held grabbed his arm with a bony hand and said, "That works for us."

"Cool." The cabby tucked the money inside his jacket and leaned back against the car to drag on his cigarette. "Lemme finish my smoke," he said through a cloud.

Leech smacked the cigarette from his lips and caught a little skin with his fingers.

"The fuck—"

"Get in the car." Leech stepped forward with such ferocity that even this grizzled veteran of the human wars recoiled and nodded, his eyes alive with worry.

"Alright, alright, let's go." He opened his door and slid

behind the wheel. Leech yanked open the back door, afraid the driver would gun the engine and take off.

The cabby drove in tense silence, tires grinding over the salted streets of Yonkers. "You gonna hit me if I light up in my own fucking cab?"

Leech tapped the smeared plastic divider. "Just crack a window."

"Please," Dr. Lotz added.

A couple of turns later and they accelerated north onto the highway.

"How fast can he move?" Dr. Lotz asked Leech.

"Not as fast as a train," Leech replied.

"Mr. Leech." Dr. Lotz's grin trembled with effort. "You lead an interesting life."

9.

The revenant thudded up the tracks in the wake of the vanishing train, as ragged as a chimney sweep. He was covered from head to foot in black ash from his dash through the tunnel and streamers of smoke rose from his shoulders.

Splinters were crushed beneath his shoes and his ragged jacket streamed in his wake. He was too slow to catch the Amtrak train once it reached speed.

He slowed to a jog and then a walk. Veering to the side of the track, he picked his way up the trash-strewn slope to a sagging chain link fence above, weaving between piles of refuse, discarded toilets and rusting bits of machinery.

He heard the whoosh of light traffic and grabbed the fence in his fingers, studying the neighborhood of row houses, parked cars, blue mailboxes and streetlights glowing to life as dusk settled her skirts over the city.

10.

Shelia Nicholson had two jobs and three children and took her personal time where she could, usually in her Jeep Cherokee listening to jazz on 88.3 FM, WBGO.

She stretched her fingers down into the blue glow of the radio dial and switched away from the news. A train had roared past not five minutes ago, going faster than it should (when you live near the tracks, you learn about the running of the railroad) but she just didn't want to know, now. She'd start her second shift soon and until then planned to enjoy the tickling of piano keys and dancing horn notes on WBGO as the sun set, watching the slow glow of the sodium lights up and down the street waking up for the night, but not in any kind of hurry.

She sensed more than saw the figure beside her window and slapped her middle finger against the glass before pushing down the door lock, her Cherokee vintage enough that it had buttons mounted beside the windows and no electric locks.

But . . .

She felt a frog in her throat and turned back, that half glimpse of his face only just registering, her cheeks going slack as she took in the ash and fungal growths and grinning white teeth.

Shelia shrieked, too slow to remember that not all of the locks were down as he hauled himself into the back seat.

"Drive."

"Get out!" she screamed, struggling to do the same. Bashing her bulk against the door without unlocking the door.

He placed one grey hand on her shoulder and she stilled, breath hitching.

"Drive or die."

A piano solo flowed from the speakers.

11.

The cab was choked with cigarette smoke and exhaust as bumper-to-bumper traffic crawled north on I-95.

"This is bigger than the Manhattan Project," Lotz said.

Instinct drove Leech north, away from Karen. Now he wish he had turned south. He needed help keeping his thoughts straight. The odd clarity that came from speaking to Karen was crumbling. He felt as if he was on the verge of something . . . something about the patients at Belmont . . . but needed her judgment to understand if it was real or his own madness shaping reality to its own warped design.

The tick-tick-tick of the turn signal snapped Leech from his reverie as the cab slid into the righthand lane.

"What are you doing?" he asked the driver, Green. "This isn't New Haven."

"We need gas and I need to drain the lizard," Green said.

"Piss later, we need to keep moving."

"Hey, fuck you, alright?" The cab picked up speed as they separated from traffic and curved along the off ramp towards the brightly lit oasis of a rest stop. "I'm not peeing my drawers for no amount of money and if we don't get gas, we won't get to New Haven."

Leech tapped Dr. Lotz on the shoulder until she grunted and said, "Where are we?"

"We're at a rest stop in Darien, Connecticut," Leech answered, loud enough to be heard up front. "The good driver has to pee."

12.

The rest stop was themed in white and blue and boasted a global array of fast food choices, from Panda Express to

Sbarro's pizza. Noise from the highway scraped at the ear in such a way that relaxing was impossible and the chaotic disarray of wandering people and revving cars felt like an experiment gone wrong.

Dr. Lotz leaned against the cab as Leech unscrewed the gas cap and inserted the nozzle from the pump. A steady chatter of sales and news snippets streamed from a speaker overhead.

Leech couldn't focus. After you lifted the curtain and looked backstage, everything started to look like a prop.

"How long is he going to be?" Dr. Lotz said, eyes fixed on the building. Leech shrugged as R&B music swelled and faded with a passing pickup truck.

"How long has Green been inside?" Leech asked.

"Nine minutes."

"Dammit." He looked around and spotted people milling around a white bus with LUCKY STAR written across the side. "How much chance is there that our driver is inside calling the police right now?"

"I don't feel well." Dr. Lotz sat down on the concrete island beside the pump.

Leech trotted across the concrete, paused to let a white Mustang rumble by, and reached the wide section of asphalt dedicated to big rigs. Three buses were parked in a slanting row like a school of massive fish caught in mid-maneuver.

He passed the PETER PAN and CHRISTIAN CHARTER to weave through the Chinese people smoking alongside the LUCKY STAR. "Where is this bus going?"

No one answered. One or two people turned away, speaking together in low tones.

He rapped the door. When it opened he placed a foot on the first step and called up to the driver, a white-haired Chinese man holding a McDonald's coffee cup.

"Are you going to New Haven?"

"Boston."

"Can we get a ticket to Boston?"

"All full." The door accordioned shut on Leech's foot and he jerked back. The crowd around him tittered.

Dr. Lotz was still seated with hands fisted into her sweatshirt pockets. Inside the hood, her forehead gleamed with sweat.

The overhead speaker said, "The Surgeon General says smoking is bad for your health, but our sign says *sale* on Marlboro Lights."

"We need to move." Leech's eyes were scanning everywhere, alighting on everything except Dr. Lotz.

They both jumped when a man's voice said, "Excuse me."

13.

Green piloted his taxi south through Darien past empty storefronts on badly lit surface streets. He recognized the signs around him. Town budget cuts meant restrictions on public lighting. He passed dark streetlights, which would irritate him if he were trying to find an address, but enveloped him in welcome shadows now.

Green thought he was better off having nothing to do with the southern fella or the sick lady. So yeah, he went inside to use the john and made a 9-1-1 call on the payphone so the fuzz wouldn't have his cell number. He got a sack of cheeseburgers from McDonald's to explain his delay but came out to find Bonnie and Clyde gone with the wind and a fat guy in an Escalade screaming at him for blocking the pump.

Fuck it, he had their cash.

He didn't notice the Jeep Cherokee on his tail until the revving engine caused him to glance in his rearview. Headlights filled the mirror with blinding light before the big vehicle accelerated past him, crossing the double yellow line as oncoming traffic honked and swerved. The

Cherokee cut back in too close and Green stood on his brakes, yanking the wheel to the right. There was a crunch of metal and glass when he slammed into a parked car outside a Midas Mufflers Shop.

"Motherfucker!"

Green shouldered open his door and yanked the sawed-off baseball bat from beneath his seat as the brake lights glowed red and the Jeep screeched to a halt.

"Are you drunk? You wanna go to jail?" Green marched stiff-legged towards the Jeep, white-knuckling the bat in his left fist.

The angle occluded his view of the passenger door but he heard the squeak of it opening and closing. The pad of feet as the driver strolled towards him and, weirdly and at first not identifiable, the sound of someone sniffing deeply. The snooty, arrogant sound of a rich prick at a wine tasting.

Green stopped mid-step, his right foot off the ground, and then retreated a bit to give himself room. He felt his bloom of rage wilting, deflating at the slow approach of the stranger and at something unseen but palpable in the air.

The red light cast the Jeep's driver in shades of crimson and black, a ragged scarecrow in bare feet with wild, fly-away hair stiffened with filth. Something was wrong with the guy's face but the white flash of his teeth was clear and unsettling.

Some kind of madman . . .

It sounded like someone was frying bacon inside the Cherokee and it took Green a moment to realize it was radio static, the volume turned up into distortion. He made out movement inside the vehicle. A lot of movement, and the Jeep abruptly roared away, leaving the stranger behind.

The blood returned to Green's knuckles as he relaxed his grip, wondering if the sawed-off bat had been seen yet, not eager to provoke any kind of retaliation from this freak. He opened his mouth. Closed it. Opened it again and asked, "Are you alright?"

A laugh like breaking glass.
"Where are they heading?"

14.

He said, "My name's Anthony," and, "It's not an Uber, it's a Doober," when he made them sit in the back seat (the front was filled with a lifetime of fast food wrappers) and sparked up a joint.

Anthony was "A Giants fan" but "The Jets are a'right" and "Those fuckin' Patriots" summed up his feeling about where they were heading. He was Dominican "But everyone thinks I'm Mexican around here," liked R&B, Rap, Reggae and smoking boo.

"You want some?" He offered the glowing cherry of the smoldering joint over his shoulder, almost scraping it out on the low ceiling of the Kia (black marks suggested this was not uncommon) and while Leech said, "No, thanks" Dr. Lotz said, "Si," and took a long hit.

"That's right, mami, you hold it, hold it," Anthony encouraged and clapped his hands with a hoot of laughter when she released an epic cloud of ganja. "Yeah, mami, yeah!"

Leech glanced at Dr. Lotz and she shrugged. "I needed something."

A short while later Anthony threw a grin back at them and said, "Yo, fuck 95, let's bust north on 15 and pick up 84 East."

"You're the man," Leech said.

"Motherfuckin' right."

15.

Leech's head was bouncing lightly against the glass as the Kia hummed north on Highway 15 and he didn't realize Anthony was exiting until he noticed the darkness of passing trees and the centrifugal pull of curving down a ramp.

"Hey!"

"Chill, bro," Anthony said. "Got to see my boy."

He slowed but coasted through a stop sign at the bottom of the ramp and turned right sharp enough to squeak the wheels.

"Huh?" Dr. Lotz started from her sleep.

"Get back on the highway," Leech growled.

"Chill." Anthony held up a hand and eased over to the shoulder. He put his elbow on the back of his seat to better turn around and look at them. "Y'all don't want no po-po, right?"

Dr. Lotz and Leech looked at each other and Anthony saw what he needed to see.

"I got twenty ounces of primo boo in the spare tire I want to leave with my boy Kevin, a'ight? We get stopped an' we get sniffed, they gon' pop all our asses. We be quick."

He smiled and Leech wondered how old he was. Twenty? Twenty one?

Leech raised an eyebrow. "You think Kevin has any pills?"

16.

They crunched over gravel in a short driveway leading to a one-story ranch house that had seen better days and parked behind a battered van with a handicapped license plate. Fingers of snow lined the driveway and clung to the black roof of the house.

"Kevin lives with his moms, she had her hips replaced," Anthony said as they pulled up. He flashed his high beams twice and turned off the engine. "He a white boy but talks like a brother, calls hisself white chocolate. You come in or stay out here?"

"We'll come."

17.

Leech waited in the cramped kitchen with Kevin and Anthony while Dr. Lotz used the restroom and the most heavenly smell on earth set his mouth to watering. As it turned out, Kevin was a veritable pharmacy and Leech felt his appetite returning along with clarity. "What kind of pizza is that?"

"White pie with clams and garlic," Kevin said, setting his plate on the table. "Moms got her slice and eats in her room, yo, watchin' her stories." An idea occurred to him. "Yo, you want a slice?"

"How much for the whole pizza?"

"Man, it just got here." Kevin gestured to the visible steam rising from the pie.

"I'll give you a hundred dollars."

Anthony punched Kevin's doughy shoulder and said, "Order yo'self another pie, dammit, and throw in a Dr. Pepper with this one."

In the end they all shared the pie on the hood of Anthony's Kia, ignoring the chill, laughing at the incongruity of it all. A joint was passed around. Ten minutes later they were back on the road.

18.

The Kia stuck to the middle lane and Anthony had a knack for finding his way into the center of a pack of cars to avoid any chance of being stopped. One highway became another and an hour passed by in Connecticut.

"Anthony." Leech leaned against the front seat.

"Yo."

"We're in a patch of trouble."

"I know."

They could see his eyes in the rearview mirror. The

only interior light was a dim orange glow from the dashboard.

"We don't just need to get to Boston. We really need to get all the way to Portland, Maine where there's a boat. Could you take us that far?"

"A'ight."

"I'll kick in an extra five hundred," Leech said.

"A'ight."

The young man fumbled through a sleeve of CDs in the door and slid a silver disc into the waiting slot on the dashboard.

"Y'all like this."

Erykah Badu sang them north.

19.

A wash of light flooded the living room windows and Kevin thumbed mute on a Jackie Chan movie in time to hear the sound of tires on the driveway.

"Moms!" Kevin heaved himself up from the couch and tugged the Islanders jersey down over the white roll of his stomach. "Pizza's here!"

He tugged a fold of cash from the baggy pocket of his sweats and peeled off a twenty and a ten—white clam pies didn't come cheap—and lumbered to the door, the floor creaking under his steps.

He stepped outside and lifted a hand against the glare of high beams. "Yo, kill the lights!"

20.

Estelle Dorsey woke herself with a snort and pushed her sliding glasses back up to the bridge of her nose, fumbling for the remote on the TV table in front of her wheelchair so she could rewind the program and see what she missed.

Her son's heavy tread drew her attention to the door as it swung open slowly. He stood in the doorway.

The light from the TV revealed that he was wearing a long, dark bib that glimmered in the flickering light.

Kevin said something wet and fell to his knees before toppling face-first into her room.

Estelle looked down at her son and back up as a raggedly dressed man filled the doorway. He bent to grab her son by the ankles and backed away, dragging the big body out into the hall, rucking up the rug beneath it.

"Kevin?" Estelle said, confused.

The revenant shouldered back into the doorway.

"Where are they headed?"

21.

All three of them were running on caffeine as false dawn drained the night's vigor, bleeding darkness until it developed the faintest pallor. Anthony followed a big rig off of the exit from Interstate 95 and when it turned right to head for the truckers' parking lot, the Kia darted left and took an open spot near the brightly lit building which boasted not only bathrooms, but a Burger King, a Popeyes, and a Starbucks.

"We'll be right back," Leech said as he helped Dr. Lotz across the nearly empty lot in the dark, moving through spheres of light and darkness in between the towering sodium lights.

Once inside they separated, peed, and met in front of the Starbucks. All it took was a look from Leech and Dr. Lotz nodded, cradling three coffees and several muffins.

When they reached the Kia, Leech said, "Got you a coffee," as Anthony unfolded from the driver's seat and stretched.

"Thanks, papi."

"Hey, leave the radio on, okay?"

Anthony nodded and leaned inside the car to stick in the key. The radio began pumping R&B as he trotted towards the building to make his own contribution to the water table and Leech made a show of leaning in the driver's side to put his coffee in the cup holder.

"He's inside," Dr. Lotz said.

Leech slid behind the wheel as Dr. Lotz eased into the passenger side, fumbling with the seatbelt. He started the engine and pulled out quickly. With no traffic in the way, he hit sixty-five before they left parking lot.

Neither of them noticed the phone jiggling around in the pocket on the driver's side door, quietly playing the theme from *Jaws*.

22.

The sky was a magical portrait in purple, pink, and yellow as the orange orb of the sun rose above the eastern horizon and their boat chugged towards the dock, a fishing trawler named SQUID INC.

"Like hope itself," Dr. Lotz said, head wreathed in marijuana smoke.

Leech held out his hand and she gave him the joint. He inhaled as if he could suck the boat to the dock more swiftly.

"I need to speak with the captain and make sure she's ready for us," Leech told her as he got out from behind the wheel. The Kia was parked beside a low metal barrier in the empty lot for DeMillo's restaurant, beyond which dozens of fishing boats rocked and swayed, Portland quiet at dawn save for the cries of lapping of the ocean and gentle bumping of boats against the docks.

Leech breathed in the salt and dead fish stink of the morning as the boat drew closer. He'd worked with the captain of SQUID INC before and shook the woman's weathered hand when she finally stepped onto the dock.

"I'll pick it up tomorrow in the usual spot," she said, her voice thick with Maine. Keen eyes raked up and down his form. "You alright?"

"I will be." Leech pushed his hat back. "Thank you again."

She winked and walked away with the short-legged, rolling gait of a lifelong sailor. Leech hustled Dr. Lotz aboard SQUID INC and in moments, the stack belched smoke and the boat eased away from the dock.

The captain produced her cell phone and hit the speed dial. "He's on the boat with the lady."

The captain's eyes widened and she stood up straight, shielding her gaze against the glare with a hand. "What the hell?" She saw the thick form slip over the stern gunwale and into the boat.

"Leech!" She broke into a run, waving her hands overhead. "SOMEONE'S ON THE BOAT!"

She spit out the cigarette and thundered to a stop as the boat left the warren of docks for the open water of Casco Bay.

23.

The chuff of the engine was loud in the hold below deck, and the slamming of the bow against the waves was the steady beat of a bass drum, filling her ears with noise. The hold itself was built very much like a closet, about five feet tall and four feet square on the bottom, enough room to make a comfortable nest out of a spare sweater and coat for Dr. Lotz. Behind her was a square hatch that opened on the main hold where the day's catch was stored.

"Thank you," she said.

"It'll be harder for Control to get their hands on you in Canada." Leech knelt by her side and held a match flame to the tip of another joint. He inhaled until it was lit and handed it to her. "We'll get you medical attention while I sort out what the hell is going on."

"You don't know what's happening?" Off his headshake. "Would you really tell me if you did?"

He dragged his finger over his breast. "Cross my heart."

She blew out a cloud of smoke and seemed to shrink a little. "What are you?"

His grin was faint but real. "Just a sick man." Darkness swallowed the hold and he spun about on his knees. "What—"

A man was silhouetted in the doorway.

"You can't tell people about us, Archie."

Leech recognized the grumbling, dry tones of the revenant and cleared his throat, straightening. "What the hell are you talking about?"

"Everything you said in your book was right." The revenant held a mossy finger to his crusted lips. "But it's need to know, dig?"

"Who are you?"

The laugh sounded like earth moving. "It's your old pal, Dick—"

Leech was drawing the Luger before the revenant finished the word.

Pain exploded against Leech's jaw as something crashed into his face. He was slammed against wooden boards when a sharp tip found the soft skin at the underside of his knee and punched up and through the meat to scrape against bone.

Leech howled as the dead thing hauled him up from the hold at the end of a boat hook, wriggling like a fresh-caught cod. The revenant backed onto the long expanse of the deck, dragging Leech after him with the boathook.

The revenant crouched, his face thunderous. A growth of mushroom closed one eye in a fungal wink. "They say catch and released doesn't hurt." He jerked the boathook free in a spray of blood and Leech wailed like a wounded animal. All thoughts of escape were drowned in the red reality of nerve endings.

The dead thing stalked away and Leech tried to press his hands over the hole behind his knee but the crimson flood squirted around his palms.

"No no no," Dr. Lotz pleaded as the revenant reappeared, dragging her by the wrist. He picked her up beneath the arms and stood her against the gunwale.

"Your kind can't know the truth," he said and she gagged at the coffin stink of his breath. "You'll drown before the sharks come." He placed a palm against her chest and pushed hard. She flipped over the gunwale and splashed into the turbulent sea, lost in the wake of the surging.

"You sonofabitch!" Leech flopped on his belly, driven by rage to pull himself towards the decaying revenant.

"We're still learning, Archie, and you told those Belmont folks too much." The revenant took the index finger of his left hand in his right fist and twisted, pulling until the digit tore free, pale strands dangling from the savaged knuckle.

"Who are you?" Leech cried out as the revenant caught his jacket in the wounded hand and drew him close with irresistible strength. "Who—"

Leech choked as the revenant stuffed his own severed finger into Leech's open mouth, pressing a hand against his lips so Leech couldn't spit it out. He struggled without success as the revenant crooned. "Eat. Eat."

The BANG was loud and the revenant jerked as a piece of his shoulder flew free. Several BANGS followed in rapid succession and Leech recognized the sound of .44 Magnums.

The shock of another boat striking their starboard side traveled through the deck of SQUID INC and men swarmed aboard, firing big .44 revolvers and swinging axes. They were dressed in the waterproof waders and filthy sweaters of fishermen, but Leech knew them for what they were.

Control.

"Spit it out," a hard-bitten man said, kneeling beside Leech and thumping him on the back. Leech coughed and chalky bits of the revenant's finger were dislodged from his throat.

"What are you doing?" Leech asked stupidly as the man tugged a fisherman's cap low over cold eyes.

"Containment," the man said, jabbing a needle into Leech's neck.

SECOND INTERLUDE

1.

THERE WAS A metal desk covered in work orders and a fan rotating inside a wall vent. A nudie calendar was the only decoration and the chugging mini-fridge was filled with beer. Dust hung in the air and the meager light came from a gooseneck lamp on the desk. It was the kind of office that would benefit from a window. The kind of office in which men grew mold.

The man in the sweat-stained shirt said, "Shooting, stabbing, burning." He spoke over the metal-on-metal sounds of the auto shop on the other side of the only door. His name was Albert and today he was the Face of Control.

Archibald Leech plucked the leg of his linen suit up from his thigh and drawled, "Cubs win the series again?" He tipped his Panama hat back and rested his feet up on the desk.

"Shut up, this is serious. Property damage, defenestration."

"Defene-what?"

"Somebody got thrown through a window."

"Right." Leech smoothed a palm down one sleeve of his summer weight jacket.

"Hey, what happened to your nose?"

"Karen." He tugged his hat brim lower.

"Right." Albert showed small teeth beneath a brush mustache.

"So this happened where, San Quentin?"

"Alaska. Cold War site."

Leech pursed his lips and shook his head. "Leave all that business buried beneath ice and time."

The chair screamed as the fat man shifted his weight forward and his forearms came down on the desk top with a meaty slap.

"Heard you got new digs."

"Yep."

"Heard you kind of trashed the other digs."

Leech remembered leaving Karen asleep on the living room couch and heading back out onto the lawn, kitchen knife in hand. Crossing the street to push through trees until he found the corrugated metal wall of their prison terrarium and followed the wall until he found a door.

He went through the door in a fit of pique and made his displeasure known to the base staff.

Vigorously.

"Karen needs fresh air," Leech said and something like liquid mercury threaded his words.

"Goddammit." Albert wiped a hand down the back of his skull. "I told them that shit wouldn't work. Fuckin' airplane hangar. You're in a good place now?"

"Good enough. Old farm. Lots of sky. Thinking about getting a couple of goats and chickens but Karen can't . . . " Leech gestured with his hand. "I need to be there to make sure they get their feed and all."

"I know you don't want to hear it, but Karen needs help. She needs to be in an inst—"

Leech blinked his eyes. That's all it took. A slammed door wouldn't have cut off the words with more authority.

A thick finger touched a nostril as if the sweating man was considering a dig to stall for time. Good manners prevented him and Albert said, "Who's picking up the tab?"

"Y'all know who's picking up the tab."

"Who's delivering the groceries?"

"You know who."

A fresh volley of sweat threaded its way up through pores on Albert's shiny head and he looked at the calendar, admiring all the faded glory that was woman. "You destroyed the place that they were keeping Karen safe and then you went haring off to Maine without sanction. You attracted a lot of attention."

Though Leech was aware of his precarious status, the attitude of louche contempt never left his face or form. "Needed a personal day," Leech said. "Mental health and all that."

The Face of Control met Leech's eyes. "You still on your personal day or are you working?"

Leech removed his hat and studied the interior as if he'd hidden an Ace of Spades inside. "Alaska?"

"By a roundabout route, yes." Albert dropped a private investigator's license on the desk and Leech took it. The fat man offered a folder operational details. It was an undercover gig, the last thing he wanted to do when his head wasn't screwed on tightly. "They can't know you're coming and we're working through outside assets." Albert looked around as if for hidden microphones. "There are leaks inside Control."

Leech slid his feet from the desk. His shoes slapped the floor like a hand against a cheek.

"Karen is gonna be pissed."

2.

The mechanics' bay echoed with the rattle and bang of wrenches as a dozen men in blue coveralls skinned their knuckles, offered curses, and practiced the art of auto repair.

Leech stepped gingerly across the oil-stained garage floor, his smooth-soled Italian shoes not much for traction in the best of circumstances. He winced at the high whine of a pneumatic tool and dug a finger in his ear to clear it out as he passed among cars in various states of dishabille.

A few of the greasemonkeys nodded as he passed and he called them by name. He stopped beside a hydraulic lift hauling a Chevy up to head height. A short Hispanic man ducked underneath and grimaced at the undercarriage.

"Ernesto."

The mechanic flicked a glance his way. "Karen hit you again?"

"Technically, it was an ashtray."

"She's loco, man."

"I need my ride."

"Bertha?"

"Si."

"Un hora." The mechanic wiped his hands on a stained rag. "Que nombre?"

The lanky man flipped open the billfold and read from the name beneath the badge. He'd argued with Control and said he didn't feel like a new goddamned name. "Archibald Leech."

"You're using the same name?"

"I told him I was tired of change."

"You picked a good one." Ernesto smiled, revealing a gap in his front teeth. "Like Cary Grant."

"Except with two Es."

Leech shook Ernesto's hand and left the garage, shoes crunching on the gravel lot. He lifted his chin to let a moist breeze fondle his neck and raised his arms as if to be crucified, the better to air out his armpits.

There was a fine green Charger built by Dodge squatting on the gravel, made no less pretty by the enormous sea of oil leaking from its private parts. It appealed to his rumrunner ancestry. He grinned around a mint-flavored toothpick, strolling around the car to run a hand along her chassis. He was a man of contradictions, high tastes and low desires, and often saw beauty where others of the linen suit set saw trash.

"Leech!"

He glanced back to see Albert waving at him from inside the garage.

"Take your damned pills!"

"Yeah, boss." Leech waved dismissively but the other man wasn't done.

"And Leech? This is a big one."

THE EIGHTH STORY

1.

"TWO MINUTES!" The bus driver pushed through the milling passengers and banged out the doors, letting in a rush of frigid air. It looked like townsfolk escaping a rising river or something from an old newsreel about European refugees.

All because there would be no dawn tomorrow.

But Leech could feel the approach of night in his marrow even as he saw it in the wide eyes around him. Already the light outside was the orange of glowing embers.

He closed the accordion doors of the phone booth to block out the chaos, people buffeting the glass in their passage. *Karen, answer the damned phone.*

Ringing in an empty house three thousand miles away. How many rings meant *I care*? At what point did that become *I panic*? At nineteen rings Leech replaced the receiver in the cradle, resting his head against the cold metal of the payphone as it regurgitated the silver. The splinted fingers on his left hand made gathering the coins awkward, but he managed.

A palm slapped against the glass and Leech looked into wet eyes glaring from an explosion of whiskers and wild hair. The man waved at him to follow and walked away without waiting.

Leech fought down an urge to try one more call and crossed the station floor, avoiding the eyes of those who remained. Big men with sloped shoulders and narrow eyes. Razors did not play much of a role in this place.

"All aboard," an announcement crackled over the antiquated public address system.

The bus belched a black cloud and took its people south.

Archibald Leech went north.

2.

The maddening light of a plummeting sun. Snow fields transformed into molten seas of blood, the trees into black ink etchings. Alien. Not even the planet Earth.

Leech kept waiting for a comment on his black eye or the purple bruise on his jaw but his driver didn't seem to notice. He pulled off the black knit watch cap and scratched his temples, but put it back on when his ears began to burn with cold. He missed his Panama hat.

The big man pulled in at a log house calling itself a saloon and led Leech to a familiar Lincoln, color: black. Bertha looked rode hard, the lower edge of her side panels grey with frozen sludge and salt. Leech hated the thought of his hairy guide driving her.

A map of Alaska was unfolded on Bertha's hood.

"You push towards Wainright." His words came in a series of grunts. Leech wondered how often he spoke to other people. A fingernail twice the thickness of a nickel traced the road until it reached a river. "You want this turnoff and you'll get a guide in, they're expecting you. Give them this."

Leech took a wrapped, rectangular package. Cash. The guide gave Leech a grin as the obvious thought showed in his face.

"I wouldn't," he said.

Leech worked his bruised jaw and ignored the implication.

"You miss it, you hit Wainright. You miss Wainright, you hit the sea."

"I won't miss," Leech said and the hairy man grunted again, plonking a rag-wrapped bundle on top of the map. Leech unfolded the checked flannel and found a greasy .38 revolver, Smith & Wesson stamped into the metal of the barrel. A box double the size of a deck of cards was filled with bullets and held an envelope in place against the rising wind.

Leech was back to his true calling.

The guide showed brown teeth when Leech asked about a phone and gestured around the side of the building. Salt and ice held the glass door of the booth shut and Leech had to hit it with his shoulder to get inside. More ringing. He dry-swallowed a couple of painkillers while he waited for the voice that didn't come.

The saloon was dark and windowless, smoke from a fireplace hanging below the ceiling and a woman's voice crooning in French from hidden speakers. The only live female in the place was running drinks to the scattered tables of hard men, her eyes marked by fatigue and fists. Leech shucked off his parka and drew stares in his wrinkled gray suit, so he slipped the coat back on. Mutters. Sidelong glances. The men here were of a piece, those who remained when humanity fled.

His broken fingers were still screaming so he said, "Bourbon, neat," hoping to drink the chill from his southern bones.

He slit the envelope with a thumbnail. Some scrawled details on the meet-up in Kwik and then a chilling sign off. *With your shield or on it*. He knew it wasn't a message from Albert. This was from the people who ran Albert. Direct from Control.

"No one does it like Edith Piaf," a man's voice crackled from the speakers and Leech heard Chicago streets in his accent. "According to the almanac, we have about three minutes of daylight left. It's gonna be a long night, people," and here the DJ paused for an uncomfortable laugh. "A real long night. Funny things happen. We start to forget about daytime, about brotherhood. The wolves will howl and we will huddle. And when you get down to the bottom and you're choosing between the taste of a bottle or a gun barrel, think about this song and make it through one more minute, all right?" He cackled again, the least reassuring radio voice Leech had ever heard. "This is radio KZXX, music at the edge of the world with, 'Here Comes the Sun'."

"That fucker," the bartender said as the song filtered through the smoke and heads dropped a little lower.

"Why do you have him on?"

"All there is." The bartender smeared the bar with a greasy rag.

Leech pulled a pack of Marlboros from an inside pocket and lipped a cigarette free, lighting it with a Zippo and then putting flame to paper. Mint tooth picks didn't cut it in Alaska.

The door bumped open and a man entered, stamping snow off his fur-topped boots. "It's here," he said quietly, and conversation stopped. In ones and twos people rose and went outside. Leech followed the bargirl through the door.

It was dark.

"Everdark," someone whispered and a ripple of agreement passed through the men, these dangerous men, who huddled closer together beneath the cloud of their breath. Some wit aimed a bright arc of urine at the building in a gesture of defiance and drew empty chuckles.

"With your shield or on it," Leech said.

"Huh?" the bargirl said, but he ignored her.

Sodium lights around the building kicked in with a snap and pushed the darkness back. Big lights, humming yellow bulbs beneath metal half domes, but they weren't nearly enough. The night was enormous overhead and all around, far larger than the great expanse of land they stood on. Alaska is said to make a man small. It reduced Leech to a speck.

He held up his hands, studying the details of knuckles and fingernails, the tape and splint. Making sure he was still here.

They were shaking with the cold.

Back inside a fight erupted and no one tried to stop it. Leech left without finishing the drink and was a half hour north before realizing he hadn't tried to call Karen.

There wouldn't be another chance until he killed the man on the radio.

3.

Bertha was a southern gal and used to a warmer climate. Her heater wasn't in shape for Alaskan ideas of cold and Leech felt the ache in his collarbone, knuckles, and ribs. Old breaks in an aging chassis singing *memento mori*.

Leech distracted himself with memories of Karen. She loved the new place, loved the grassy slopes and had brought up the notion of getting a few animals before he did.

The memories made him long for home, but they distracted him from the cold.

4.

Bertha rumbled across a long, arching bridge with nothing but the void on either side.

Night. The word took on new meaning.

Even in the suburbs there were streetlights, the distant glow of town. But once the sun went down in the nowhere, the world was reduced to the cone of light from the headlights. It was insignificant, that light. As inadequate as all of his preparations.

"That was 'Ode to Joy' by," the DJ sucked in a lungful of smoke, voice strained, "by Beethoven, man, dig it. Nothin' to do in the dark except listen, that's what I'm doing and I'm glad you are, too."

The DJ took shape in Leech's mind as he drove, growing long and lizard-like in his studio, attached at the mouth to the serpentine hose of a Moroccan hookah. He'd be filthy. Uncombed hair the color of ashes and bad skin that never saw a bar of soap.

"And now we're gonna let our hair down with m'man Clapton and 'Sunshine of Your Love'."

"Are you kidding me?"

The DJ cackled in response.

Rock, classical, and then some tribal stuff with drums. In between he rambled and ranted about anything that came to mind. Religion. Communism. A divorce, presumably his. This guy was higher than a kite and the only radio station on the air. How did he get such range?

"They don't know, they don't know, man, lemme tell you, *they know*. Your new HD-TV with voice control? It's always listening, even when you turn it off. Think about that, man. You like to jerk off to Internet porn? Man I hope you cover that camera with some tape because they can see you. Yeah, yeah. They say they don't know how many people cops kill every year? Of course they know, they don't want you to know but they know. They know everything and they like it." He took a breath to cough and Leech could hear the static-laden suck of a pipe. "Know what they don't like? I know what they know. I can hear them in their little bunkers and they hate it."

As granddad would say, he was crazier than a shithouse rat.

"This will be a humanitarian gesture," Leech said and Johnny Cash answered by singing he once shot a guy in Reno.

Leech was getting squirrelly. Popping too many

painkillers and doing everything he could not to think about the phone ringing with no one to answer. After years of saying, "Yessir," and, "How high?" maybe it was time to haul stakes.

He had enough dough stuffed in various accounts to get Karen down to Mexico where the dollar went far and the tequila flowed like liquid gold. He wouldn't be able to use any of his identities, but he knew people in low places that could hook them up with paperwork, make them Mr. and Mrs. Smith. Get a place near the water and be around to make sure Karen didn't swim when she shouldn't.

He was picturing her in the surf when the fire blazed up on his right and Bertha flashed past, unaware until he hit the brakes that Bertha was doing eighty miles an hour. She fishtailed to a screeching stop and he threw the gearshift into reverse, backing up with a high whine of the engine into the crimson glow of taillights. Bertha jerked to a stop in front of a collection of low structures surrounding a bonfire.

The dome light came on when Leech shoved open the door, the loneliest nightlight on the planet. Squinting helped him make out shapes moving around the fire, wide and lumbering things leaking a high-pitched chant. Dogs were howling.

He leaned back inside Bertha to see a red light glowing on the dashboard.

Control had not released the Activator.

"Damn you."

He closed the door carefully, as if Bertha's roar had not already announced his presence. When the dome light went dark he felt like he had burned a bridge behind him.

Wind whistled and he hunched his shoulders around his ears, sliding a hand into his coat pocket to touch the frozen hunk of metal that was his only weapon. A .38? The frozen waste beneath its shroud of night was home to wolves and bears and phantoms conjured by his uneasy mind and he wondered if the stubby brass cartridges in his revolver would do much more than irritate a beast into a greater paroxysm of violence.

His shoes crunched across the crust of snow and ice as he approached the collection of low-slung structures with wooden frames and hide walls that shimmered and flapped in a weird approximation of life. An Inuit place. He stepped close to one and touched it, wincing at the grease and stink, listening to the rhythmic grunting from within when a hand slapped against the hide from the inside.

He gasped as fingers dug through the hide to trap his own and he was shocked at their strength. He was yanked against the greasy animal skin barrier before he could set his feet and felt a hard punch to the gut.

"What?"

He staggered backwards and the spear followed him, its wooden half emerging from the hole in the tent like an extruded tongue, the sharp head driven through his winter goat and buried in his stomach.

He was still connected to the tent by the umbilicus of the spear shaft when strong fingers grabbed his hair from behind and yanked his head back. A line of ice was drawn across his throat and a majestic spray of blood arced from his opened throat.

And it was like that, blood arcing over like a red rainbow, knees only just unhinging, that the moment seized and Leech did not fall. Reality froze and shook like an old VHS tape on PAUSE.

5.

Leech was picturing Karen laughing in the surf when the fire blazed up on his right and Bertha flashed past it, unaware until he hit the brakes that Bertha was doing eighty miles an hour. She fishtailed to a screeching stop and he threw the gearshift into reverse, backing up with a high whine of the engine into the crimson glow of taillights. Bertha jerked to a stop in front of a collection of low structures surrounding a bonfire.

The dome light came on when Leech shoved open the door, the loneliest nightlight on the planet. Squinting helped him make out shapes moving around the fire, wide and lumbering things leaking a high-pitched chant. Dogs were howling.

He leaned back inside Bertha to see a red light glowing on the dashboard.

Control had not released the Activator.

Leech pictured the Face of Control, sweat rolling in greasy beads from beneath his oiled comb over. Who was he to make decisions? Leech was the man sent out into the Void. Leech.

He tugged up the cuff of his right pant leg, reaching inside his sock. The folding Buck knife was warm from contact with his skin and opened eagerly. Leech wriggled out of his parka, ignoring the sudden bite of cold as he stretched his body along Bertha's wide front seat and gently rested his fingers against the tiny console holding the Activator. He held his breath before releasing it through his nose, consciously slowing his heart rate.

Thirty-seven seconds later a spark leapt from the tip of his probing knife and Bertha exploded.

Reality froze and shimmered.

6.

Ragged clouds of breath puffed from Leech's mouth like the smoke from a failing locomotive. His lungs were fire and his feet blocks of ice, the revolver an empty vessel he dropped as he fled the Inuit village.

The plain before him was an unending silver sea and had the dogs not been so close on his heels, the lunar beauty might have struck him as magnificent. The moon was a cool spectator overhead and Leech wanted to be there on its pocked surface or swimming in Caribbean water or anywhere that wasn't this frozen plain of death.

Snarls leaked from the pursuing pack and the Inuit rifles had gone silent, sure that there was no escape for the white man from the south, simply waiting for him to realize it.

And he did.

Skidding to a stop he slipped, shards of snow and ice pattering down around him. He turned to see the low-slung shapes of the onrushing hunters and thought this was a terrible way for his story to end.

"Cut!" he shouted, jabbing a finger at the lead dog.

He was hit by three dogs at once, the powerful Huskies flattening Leech as the pack arrived and tore him to shreds.

7.

Leech was picturing her in the surf when the fire blazed up on his right and Bertha flashed past it, unaware until he hit the brakes that Bertha was doing eighty miles an hour. She fishtailed to a screeching stop and he threw the gearshift into reverse, backing up with a high whine of the engine into the crimson glow of taillights. Bertha jerked to a stop in front of a collection of low structures surrounding a bonfire.

The dome light came on when Leech shoved open the door, the loneliest nightlight on the planet. Squinting helped him make out shapes moving around the fire, wide and lumbering things leaking a high-pitched chant. Dogs were howling.

A chime sounded behind him and he leaned back inside Bertha to see a green light glowing on the dashboard.

Control had released the Activator.

A moment of rebellion stayed his hand. The thought of

his brain chemistry dancing to Control's tune offended him, but he knew he needed its release. It's activation and leaned back in the car—

The radio squealed to life and the tuner spun through the stations. A cacophony of voices assaulted him and the delicate balance of his inner ear spun like a wild compass. He was consumed by an avalanche of déjà vu. He felt himself standing and falling and laying and speared and bitten and—

Leech was on his knees beside Bertha, safe within the glow of her dome light. He shuddered and sucked in air, unsure when he had last drawn breath. That something profound had just happen, was happening, was certain. That he was not directing the course of events was also certain . . .

Not directing.

Not directing.

Not directing.

Ten thousand miles away, he stood in a laboratory in the town of Durable, Arkansas and stepped through a door.

(WHITE)

The sky cracked overhead and thunder rumbled.

It was as clear and real a moment as the present, where blood from his nostrils dripped onto his lips and his mouth tasted like pennies. He remembered the door opening. The scientists shrinking back as he stepped through

(WHITE)

Brilliant jags of lightning ripped the night sky like the claws of god.

He stepped through

(Not directing)

He stepped through the door

(Not directing)

He stepped through the door backstage and saw how the magic happened.

In Alaska, the wind went still.

In Durable, or as close as Durable was to that other
(WHITE)
Archibald Leech had his audition with the Director.
The air popped and he was in Alaska and only Alaska where the sky was onyx and the ground was mercury.
The quiet pop lingered, growing louder as it traveled farther away and Leech let his mind free in the Ever Dark, twisting through his many stories as a galaxy of neurons lit up like forked lightning across his brain. Activator? Control didn't activate him. Control kept him down, in a cage. A mind cut off from itself.
He thought of dead Dr. Lotz and undead Dick Wilkes. He remembered a brave little man named Jeffs swinging a burning torch and the shivering bulk of the gargantuan mushroom in a dark chamber. He heard the tearing fabric of reality in doomed Durable and opined that the witness to such events must be something, all right. What had Karen said about his special mind?
Archibald Leech activated.
Dreaming Titans rolled over in their sleep and the electric capillaries of the stratosphere glowed like filaments. He wondered why he had ever hesitated to fill his mind with fire.
The stars bled light overhead as he headed in amongst the buildings. He knew that if he turned around, he would see his own trail of light and wondered what the stars thought.
He nearly walked into a building while his activated brain danced. He could be here in the now or fully Activated, but not both at once.
Focus on the job at hand.
The village was little more than a collection of low-slung structures with wooden frames and hide walls that shimmered and flapped in a weird approximation of life. An Inuit place. He stepped close to one and touched it, wincing at the grease and stink, listening to the rhythmic

grunting from within when a hand slapped against the hide from the inside.

The tip of a spear punched through and he twisted aside, snatching the wooden shaft behind the bone head and yanking it free, stepping back and dropping to one knee as he swung it in a wide arc and batted a knife from the hand of a heavily bundled Inuit creeping up behind him.

The woman squawked and backpedaled, falling on her ass and clutching her stinging hand. Leech rose and stood looking down at her as fear flashed through her eyes.

"Ma'am." He offered his hand and hauled her to her feet. He held out the spear to her and she took it, but made no move to resume aggression and he touched the brim of his black watch cap.

The smell of charred meat was strong on the air and the chant continued as he moved past the outer ring of structures and into the central circle where the strange silhouettes sang and swayed. A carved post rose out of the fire, the faces of unrecognizable animals bellowing silently all the way up to a winged shape at the top. Why it wasn't consumed by the blaze he couldn't tell but a bundle wrapped in chains was attached to it, shapeless and blackened, dripping fat visible as it trickled into the fire.

It occurred to him that jogging back to Bertha and cranking her up to full speed might be the wise play. Skip the mission and move south until he could slip into the Lower Forty-Eight. Pick up Karen and head for that imagined beach.

He discarded the idea immediately. He was on thin ice after the Lotz incident and the damage he did to the terrarium. Control wanted him on the job or . . .

Dead?

The word popped into his head and once it did, he couldn't shake it. He thought about what happened to animals that escaped their cage.

Did Control see him as a liability?

Was he supposed to come back from this one?

"Qui etes-vous?"

He spun at the words, hand jammed into his pocket where he had the .38.

A bundled figure emerged from the nearest building, the hide entrance slapping closed before Leech could see anything but a faint glow inside. She was short and wide in a seal skin coat trimmed with fur. Her cheeks glistened with bear-fat, framed by pendulous black braids.

"What?"

The chanting stopped as if he'd tripped a switch. Long-haired women gathered in between Leech and the fire. Squat in their native winter gear, a museum display come to life. They held spears tipped with white bone and despite their numbers regarded him with widened eyes and trembling weapons.

"English? Do you speak English?" Leech asked, looking back and forth between the crowd and his questioner. A woman detached herself from the group and said something full of liquid clicks before approaching.

"Why are you here?" Her words strangely accented. She was a full head shorter than him, eyes narrow in a round face.

"I'm Leech. I'm supposed to meet my guide, take me to KZXX. The radio station."

That eerie liquid tongue spilled from a dozen mouths and the English speaker turned to them, shouting and slashing the air with her hand. She turned back as the group quieted and said, "Not good there, not good for men."

"I don't understand."

"Dark." She waved overhead to encompass the starry sky. "Sound." She opened her mouth to wail in that disconcerting way. The women behind her took up the chant and spread out to circle the fire again. "Sick." She stepped close enough for him to smell the onions on her breath as she tapped his temple with a blunt finger.

Leech thought of the people who had stayed behind to the south, almost all men. The sense of despair. The fight at the bar.

"Go home," the woman said.

"Can't."

She snorted and shook her head, the beads at the end of her braids clacking. She held out her hand and Leech pulled the thick bundle of money from his pocket. She jerked her head in a "follow me" gesture and set off around the dancers.

The chanting took on a grating quality as he drew closer and he had the crazy idea that with a little effort he'd understand it. That understanding it was a bad idea. The sound of an invisible ant scratching inside his ears until he chanced to look up at the cooking bundle on the pole.

Christ. No wonder he frightened them.

"Come," the guide barked and he shook himself into motion. He crunched through the snow after her, slip-sliding in his smooth-soled shoes as she hurried past a row of tied-up dogs that snarled and snapped at their passage.

"Dog sled?" Leech said and she snorted in disdain before pulling the tarp from a snow mobile with an incongruously yellow fuselage. She straddled the long seat and waved impatiently for him to climb on behind her, forced to press against the feral stink of her clothing. She gunned the machine to roaring life and twisted the throttle several times, blotting out the awful chanting with the mechanical roar.

Even as the machine lurched forward and his toes dragged in the snow, Leech couldn't resist a last look at the charred shape broiling over the bonfire, struck by the shocking whiteness of the man's familiar face.

His face.

6.

The snowmobile rattled and buzzed recklessly through an evergreen tunnel with the looming trees on either side and branches interlocking overhead. Sight was minimal, the narrow cone of brilliance thrown by the snowmobile's single headlight an invitation to disaster. The sound was a deafening pressure against Leech's ears, his eyes watered and his cheeks burned from the frozen dagger of the wind. Every muscle in his body screamed in protest as he hung on for dear life, whipped from side to side and slammed down with teeth-rattling force.

Never stopping. Never slowing.

The headlight flashed off metal in the trees but they were past before he could make it out. Ground opened to the right and a vast, circular shadow rose against the starry sky. The Inuit woman slowed to swerve in between domes of concrete. Three great obelisks. It was a haunted high-tech landscape of metal and ice that had no place in the Alaskan wilderness.

Leech felt the slide of his sanity. His consciousness. Something pulled at him, dancing with the Activator to stroke the untapped potential of his mind to life.

He saw the white of a burned man's eyes and felt the awful heaviness of a month-long night. In his ears liquid singing keened against the murmuring voice of a madman riding a cannabis high and over it all the buzzing of the mechanical steed that carried him ever north—

Leech slammed the broken fingers against his thigh and the wind snatched away his cry of pain. Reality reasserted itself.

The machine slid to a stop and she switched off the engine. The silence pounded in his ears and beneath the inner thunder he heard a murmuring voice that was not his own. In the last flicker of the headlamp Leech saw a large bundle hanging from a tree, its lower edges sprouting crimson icicles.

"What have you done?"

The dark settled around them like a giant's hand and Leech fought the urge to crouch, to hide. The ticking of the engine was loud and unnatural against the susurrus of breeze and branch, the crunch of snow as his guide moved purposely about the snowmobile removing items from saddlebags. When Leech moved to get out of her way the murmuring grew louder and he realized a voice spoke on the night wind.

"What is that?"

What he thought were wind-blown flakes turned out to be the outriders of a storm and Leech wondered if he would get snowed-in after he did this thing.

"Hey." He staggered as she shoved a cloth-wrapped bundle against his belly. "What is this?"

"Give to him," she said and unlimbered a rifle from a tube that ran along the length of the machine. She slung it over her shoulder with easy familiarity. "Follow."

"I can't see anything."

"No light. Follow."

He glanced back at an eerie yip-yip-yip drifting through the trees from the direction of the concrete towers. The sound wasn't repeated and he turned back to find his guide nearly vanished in the forest ahead.

The wind and snowfall picked up as she led him through the trees towards a glowing red light. The voice defined itself, clarified into the rambling cadence of the DJ riding a hundred speakers hung throughout the trees. It was a maddening sound, the voices slightly out of synch due to distance so that some words continued long past their allotted time and others were chewed and dragged under by the chorus. Some words ringing clear but the larger meaning obscured just enough to lure a listener forward in search of understanding.

A snow-covered hump up ahead turned out to be a squat building made of concrete and native logs, as if it had been expanded ad hoc since its original construction. A giant metal radio tower rose beside it but other than that, details were hard to make out.

The red light was a sign over the front door, the familiar words out of place in this remote wilderness:

ON AIR.

7.

Twice Leech lifted his hand to knock on the metal door but hesitated, as well trained as any dog not to make noise while the ON AIR light was on overhead. He turned around to say something to the woman, but the woods were empty save for the echoing voices.

"This is stupid," he said and knocked on the door, three sharp raps that hurt his knuckles. It was solid as hell, like striking a fifty-five gallon drum full of ice. Leech wondered if the man inside heard him over the din of horns that filled the forest, Wagner maybe.

Leech was lifting his hand to knock again when the door opened to bathe him in orange light. He felt a warm puff of air. A little man with a wild beard, Hawaiian shirt, and cargo shorts grinned up at him.

"Hey Archie, I'm Don," he said in that familiar voice. "Nice to meetcha." Leech caught the odor of marijuana and buttered popcorn riding on the tropical air currents. "Come in and warm—"

Leech pulled the pistol from his coat pocket, thumbed back the hammer, and shot Don in the chest.

It made a flat bang. A horrible sound. It seemed as if the music should've stopped but it didn't, continuing to wail and thrash as Don sat down and his teeth clacked. He winced as if that hurt, the teeth, then flopped onto his back, mouth working like a suffocating fish.

The hole in his chest was a low-pressure faucet pumping thick syrup. Leech stepped inside that comforting miasma of weed and popcorn (a black and white movie was playing on a TV in the corner) and jabbed the .38 down at Don's contorting face before pulling the trigger. His forehead collapsed as if slapped with a hammer and a spray of blood-veined oatmeal spilled across the floor. A wet fan of all that he had ever thought and been and Leech fired again, the bullet taking him through the gawping mouth, .38 caliber fellatio and Leech shot him again and would have shot him until the sun burned cold and the earth was finally consumed by the everdark but the gun was empty, the cylinder rotating dutifully with each pull of the trigger, the hammer uttering its oily snap, snap, snap.

A rushing wind swept through Leech's mind as he dropped the gun, turning and tottering out into the rosy glow of the ON AIR light, not fleeing so much as stumbling from the scene of the crime. The murder.

He didn't understand his reaction. He'd killed more people than—

Leech was turning back to pick up the revolver when flames reached from the tree line and invisible fingers plucked at his coat. Thunder rumbled as splinters threw themselves from the log walls. Sparks illustrated the meteoric impact of bullet against door as Leech looked over his shoulder, not comprehending the moving shadows and muzzle flashes. Low shapes trailing snarls as they flew across the snow, dogs with dripping fangs charging with predatory speed.

Lurching inside, Leech tripped over his victim as automatic fire blasted all around the door and sent flaming metal wasps darting over his head. He thought, *They have a machine gun!* even as he kicked the door shut and scuttled backwards to land in the moist smear of Don's offended skull.

Breathing hard as the wet seeped through his pants, he read the warning spray-painted on the inside of the door:

BEWARE DEAD AIR

The operatic music quieted and in the silence he heard no more gunshots, was instead absurdly concerned at the thought of dead air and turned, the seat of his pants sliding in gore. He looked around the endless shelves of record albums covering every wall and heard the old fashioned clicking of a record player as a ghost hand lifted the needle to one side.

A tiny green LED lit up on an engineer's panel of dials and switches and a cassette engaged. "Hey now," the disc jockey's voice filled the room. "I can't think of a better way to end the show than 'Ride of the Valkyries', can you? And what an ending of the show this is, cats and kittens. The *end* end. The Big D. That long awaited day has come and it's time for me to go off the air. But don't worry! I'm leaving you in the care of a man who will treat you right, come all the way from Chicago to make magic on the airwaves—I'm talking to you, baby, start with turntable two."

Leech looked past an elaborate record press to the turntables lined up like a weird devolutionary display from the Museum of Broadcasting, starting from a high-tech digital job and going all the way back to an old Victrola with a giant brass speaker horn.

"Everybody give it up for Archibald Leech!"

Applause drowned out the DJ's voice until silence filled the room when the tape clicked off. He crossed the studio in three great strides and turned the power knob on the second turntable until it popped and he heard a feedback *thumpf* over the speakers. The slightly warped record began to spin and he lifted the needle, lowering it into the outer groove.

"JEREMIAH!" The shout filled the room and Leech ducked as the speakers continued bellowing, eyes raking across the annotated index cards taped hither and yon across the control panel. He saw one marked *In-Studio Volume* and spun the dial, bracing his hands on the console as the singing dropped to a dull roar.

"What the fuck?" Leech was a broken record, repeating it over and over. "What the fuck?"

A black chair on wheels was turned to face him and a Memorex cassette tape sat on the cushion with an index card on it. Cheerfully round loops of magic marker spelled out: ARCHIE, PLAY ME.

Leech turned the plastic cassette over and over in his hands and was still doing so as "Joy to the World" faded from the speakers.

Dead air again.

"Shit."

Leech snapped off the power knob and grabbed a boom mic dangling at the end of a telescoping arm, tore off the index card commanding TALK INTO ME and flipped a switch at the base from OFF to ON.

"This is Archie Leech," he said. *Archie?* "Coming to you from the great white north. It's been a strange day, my friends, one strange f—" He caught the curse before it escaped on air, "—darned day, really weird, but there's dead air and everyone knows we can't have dead air so here it is—" A flailing hand picked up an album and he shook it from the sleeve, whipping *Three Dog Night* off of the turntable and dropping the new record in its place. "'I Wanna Be Your Dog' from the one and only, Iggy Pop."

Fuzzy guitars filled the air as Leech picked up the cassette with his name on it and stuck it into a tape player. Checked to make sure it was only an area speaker and hit play.

"Hey Archie, I know you've got a million questions, not the least of which is how I know your name . . ."

"No shit," he told the control panel.

" . . . but you gotta listen to me now, right fucking now." The hippy tones were gone and Don sounded intense, even scared. "First thing is, never let the dead air last. The music keeps everything calm down below. Second, by now you've figured out those Eskimo bitches won't let you leave. They think you're infected. Get it through your head, amigo, you're *never* gonna leave. Ever."

"Says you."

"And last, but definitely not fucking least: drag my body down into the cellar. Keep going down through the subbasements as far as you can go until you find the well, understand? Throw my body in the well. Your life depends on it."

Leech looked at the corpse resting in a gummy pool of blood.

"Oh, Archie, if I say anything down there—don't answer."

8.

"You don't have much time," Don's voice crackled over the old, Walkman headphones. "And there's a lot you need to know."

A bare bulb swung back and forth on a cord overhead and Leech's shadow danced as he dragged the body down the steps, wincing at each cruel thud of the head on wood. The staircase rocked beneath him and descended towards a weird, blue glow. He was sweating from more than just the cloying humidity and he paused to take off his jacket, draping it over the railing. He untangled his tie from the headphones cord and tossed it over one shoulder.

"You're gonna get a call soon, whoever they're holding over you," the DJ continued. "Probably Karen, right?" A wave of cold washed through Leech when the dead man said her name. "They're gonna hurt her, make her scream, man. But they won't kill her yet because they want something from you, something only you can give them."

Would Control really call? Of course they'd call. They'd have a Plan B in case the Inuit assassins failed.

Dark stains were soaking through the blanket wrapped around the body and he was relieved when his shoes scraped on the gritty concrete of the floor.

"I left instructions for you upstairs." Feedback squealed on the tape and Leech reached for the Walkman on his belt. A blue spark of static electricity stung his hand. ". . . tell you how to listen with the dishes, where to listen to give them what they want. I'll say it again, with this place, you can eavesdrop on just about any electronic conversation in the world, man, dig it? That's what they want. The G-Men, but here's the thing, I tried to tell them but they don't care . . . "

He paused.

"It only lets you listen to poison, something that means bad news for someone. It doesn't just *want* ugliness, it needs it. Sucks it down through those big dishes and radio arrays like a junkie."

Leech turned and saw row upon row of leafy marijuana plants arrayed beneath sapphire-tinged grow lights. "You're kidding me."

The madness began to make some kind of sense.

Don spoke through a smoker's cough. "Now, quick, find the next cassette and do what I say." The tape ended and the PLAY button on the Walkman popped up.

Leech wanted to sit down and laugh until he cried, to pull off a couple leaves from old Mary Jane and chew them until he drifted away. This was too strange and getting more so by the minute. But he'd scared Leech, this DJ who knew his name. Scared Leech enough that he was following a dead man's voice down into the frozen bowels of the earth.

You don't have much time. Right.

The perfume of the plants was thick in his nostrils as he moved through the blue light between towering bushes, stepping over a coil of hose before he found what he was looking for.

Leech pushed aside shovels and other long-handled tools to reveal a heavy steel door set into the sweating wall. Some kind of disabled security card reader was mounted beside it.

UNAUTHORIZED ENTRY FORBIDDEN BEYOND THIS POINT was a faded stencil on metal.

He leaned a shoulder into the door and pushed because there was no way to pull. It was only by accident that he discovered the door was designed to slide to one side. After a moment of effort it opened and he jerked away from the rain of rust.

A plastic clatter caught his attention and Leech picked up another cassette, feeding it into the Walkman and tossing the first tape into the basement jungle.

The audio whirred to life as Leech trotted back through the plants. Static. Sounds of movement. He stood over Don's body, trying to figure out the best place to grab hold when a dead hand had slipped free from the blanket cocoon. Leech struggled with the bizarre idea that he was acting in the present while listening to a voice recorded only a matter of hours earlier. Time was splitting.

Time slide. His head was splitting open, glowing antennae unfurling to read the air. He felt like he'd been zapped with a double shot of Activator.

Don's voice kicked in: "Stop fucking around, man. Get my body through the door and down to the well, now!"

Panic in the DJ's voice. "Do you know that guy who picked you up at the bus station? He called Salvatore to let him know you were on the way. Right now while I'm talking into a microphone you're driving north to kill me. Far out." A choking sound and Leech imagined tears.

"Look, man, I don't blame you. I knew this would happen when I threatened to play the record. Maybe I wanted it to happen, I'm so damned lonely up here." He laughed through his tears. "I mean, if I really wanted to end the world I would have just played the fucking record, right?"

"What record?" Leech asked the ghost.

"Enough messing around, get my body, man, do it. You really have to move."

Leech grabbed the feet and walked backwards, dragging the corpse through the dark opening.

9.

The next set of overheads flickered reluctantly to life and Leech let out a harsh breath. The lights always took an extra few seconds before the motion sensors triggered. He was overcome with an onslaught of nyctophobia while David Bowie sang over the tinny PA system. He thought the Alaskan night had taught him about darkness. What a child. True darkness was underground where the sun didn't exist.

"Put on a stack of records and let 'em play through. Keep track of the records, of the time," the DJ had instructed. Bowie meant that Leech still had plenty of time. He wondered if this was how he would sleep in days to come, dependent on a stack of records.

His laugh fell flat in the bizarre tunnel with its nonsensical letters and numbers beside doors he was told to ignore. The tunnel itself was ribbed and lined with tubes whose function he could only guess at. The whole thing designed by someone who thought *The Jetsons* meant the future.

"Keep going, Archie, keep walking through the fear," my old friend on the radio was saying. "I know you're freaking out, I sure as hell was. Like they built this place to give a guy the heebie jeebies, so deep with no air. And man, how the sound falls flat, right?"

Was Don fucking with him?

"But you gotta get me down to that well, so find those stairs and ignore everything but my voice from this point on, no matter how weird things get."

Mounted on the wall Leech saw fire extinguishers. Axes. Coiled hoses. Something marked a DECON STATION. Everything rusty. His broken fingers were throbbing and his nose ran from the clouds of dust he kicked up.

The body rasped along the floor as he pulled it into another inky spill of shadow and hesitated.

The light overhead buzzed into radiance but never found its stride and flickered madly as Leech hurried beneath it. His ears filled with the sound of his own ragged breath and he wondered where Don—

"I know you're freaking out, hold it together." Leech heard him inhaling deeply. "Let me tell you about this place, this damned place that was never used after millions of dollars and seven people—*seven*—died during construction." Leech heard him blowing, imagined the cloud of smoke until Don resumed with a crackle. "It was the Cold War, man, and the military wasn't going to listen to anyone, especially not a bunch of fucking Eskimos with their fucking legends about a bad place. A hungry place. *Perlertok tonrar*."

Leech stood up straight as a sound rolled down the corridor. Someone giggling.

"Hungry Devil is what they called this place, a place that makes men sick. But the military dug and dug and woke it up, gave it the tools to amplify its reach. Boost the devil's signal, man, can you dig that?"

Leech bent back to his burden when Don screamed in his ears and he jumped. "THEY MADE IT STRONGER! IT CAN REACH AROUND THE WORLD AND TWIST THINGS, TURN THINGS AND MAKE PEOPLE DIE."

Leech dragged Don with his uninjured hand while the sweat poured down his face his hair became a salty swamp. A laugh bounced off the walls from somewhere behind him as one by one, the lights back there went dark.

"Hey Archie, Archie?"

The voices were dopplering and Leech realized that Don wasn't speaking through the headphones. He lifted a padded earpiece and cocked an ear at the nearest PA speaker, but the voice wasn't coming from there either.

"Don't throw me down the well, it's so cold down there."

Every muscle went rigid as Leech stared at the blanket-shrouded body.

"Let's go back up and smoke awhile," the voice wheedled from beneath the blanket.

"Oh shit," Leech said and if he hadn't found the door marked STAIRS just then, he would have run. But there it was and he ripped it open. Dragged the corpse through until the heavy metal door swung closed on the head and they were stuck. He pulled viciously until the skull squeezed through with a wet crunch.

It was like stepping from a steam room into a meat locker and Leech fell against the door, shivering as a yellow lamp on the wall buzzed to life. The metal burned with cold and he pulled away, breath clouding. He felt an eerie constriction on his temples as short hairs froze.

Black veins of ice lined the walls and Leech slipped on a slick stair, jarring the breath from his lungs when he fell. The body tobogganed down the stairs until it crashed at the landing and spilled free from the blankets. The impact was so great and the icy concrete so slippery that the corpse rebounded around the corner and teetered on the edge of the next flight down. "No . . . " Leech moaned before it was sucked down and out of sight.

Rubbing at his abused back, Leech picked his way down the stairs, fingers growing numb on the metal railing while the voice in his ear spouted delusions and kept him company.

" . . . part of the Distant Early Warning Line, get it? Code named White Bear. Things went wrong before they put the system online, all those construction deaths, but once they cranked up those dishes everyone with a pair of headphones got sick." Leech touched his own headphones involuntarily and looked down the next flight as the weak overhead lamps lit themselves. The blanket lay in a heap on the landing below but the body had continued its careening slide and vanished around the right-angled turn for the next set of descending stairs.

"When the month-long night came, they went crazy. Started seeing Russian bombers every time the wind changed direction. Pushed us to Defcon Two half a dozen times before Washington figured out there was a problem with the site. Then the operators up here started killing each other and, well, can you imagine that meeting at the Pentagon?" He wheezed and Leech realized Don was laughing. "Sorry, General, looks like we should have listened to the natives. White Bear is haunted."

Leech followed an organic smear down flight after flight beneath the inadequate lights until he was uncertain how deep beneath the earth's surface he had traveled. He blocked out his companion's voice, worry increasing as the precise, government stenciling on the walls grew looping and stick-like. At first the symbols were recognizable as letters and numbers but the shapes grew more distorted the further down he went, until he couldn't identify them at all.

There, the body was piled against the door to the next subbasement only one more flight below.

The PA system went silent as Leech reached the dead man and he waited, teeth chattering violently, listening anxiously to the whir and click of another record dropping into place over the PA system. A liquid clicking crackled from the speakers and then a horrible keening filled the air. It was a song sung by fleshless mouths, mandibles and teeth clicking together beneath a strange, warbling chant. The same as that sung by the Inuit women around a bonfire while they cooked a man alive.

Leech cast about wildly as if the strangely marked walls would offer some explanation, tell him how those murderous hags had replaced the next album. Were they waiting above with guns and dogs? Were they trying to frighten him onward where a final subbasement contained a devil?

Leech turned to flee upstairs, done with their games.

He made it to the first step when a cold hand gripped his ankle.

10.

Leech squeezed the sponge in both hands and pink, frothy water cascaded back into the bucket. A smoldering joint dangled from his lips and he blinked against the rising curl of smoke as he resumed scrubbing at the mess inside the door. The broken fingers barely hurt at all.

He heard a voice, not the radio, and glanced at the old brown door that opened on an unsteady flight of wooden stairs down to the basement.

"Shut up, you're down in the well." He eyed the bloody fire axe leaning against the door, remembering the nightmare struggle in the subbasement.

It had taken three great whacks at the joint of neck and shoulder with the fire axe before Don's head had bounced free, still gibbering as it tumbled down the slippery stairs. Leech was hurrying after it when, to his horror, Don's headless body rose and stumbled down the stairs in blind pursuit.

Leech hit the bottom level at a run and nearly charged headlong into the well, which was less a well than a great, gaping hole surrounded by a circle of jagged rocks. He threw his weight backwards and his feet shot out from under him so that he landed hard, jarring his tailbone. He slid to within a foot of the well and was blinking tears from his eyes when the blind corpse staggered off the last step and into the chamber, arms swinging about and hands clutching as it tottered straight towards him, homing in with a sense that he couldn't understand.

Leech pivoted to his left and swung out a foot to trip it.

It plunged into the well without a sound. He never heard the corpse strike bottom.

Leech stood warily, breath whistling from tortured lungs. He glanced around the natural cavern, lit in a strange green glow by veins of lichen that grew up from the well to swarm across the walls and arch across the ceiling.

He returned his study to the well, a black maw surrounded by sharp stones that reminded him of so many jagged teeth.

"Don't do it, man," Don's voice issued from the dark, words mushy from a broken jaw. Leech found the head tucked beside a stone.

He picked it up in both hands, turning it until he could stare into the milky, cataract-covered eyes. It tried to smile and the effect was grotesque.

"It gets so lonely here, you have to believe me. Bring me back upstairs. You could mount me on a turntable and let me spin around while we talk about records."

"Shut up, Don."

Teeth snapped at his thumb. Leech shoved the head away from him with a cry of disgust and it bounced across the stony floor. Before Don could speak again, Leech stepped forward and scooped the head towards the well with a sweeping kick, as if passing a soccer ball. The head struck a stone and bounced into the air but momentum spun it forward and it tumbled into the black cavity screaming curses.

Leech spat on the stone floor.

"Tell the Hungry Devil that Archibald Leech sends his regards."

II.

The wind howled against the building and Don's collection of homemade, shiny steel records rattled on the walls.

In the cramped kitchen he washed dirt from his hands

and filled a saucepan with water, carrying it back into the radio studio where he had dragged one of the marijuana plants. He soaked the dirt, spilling water across the floor. He'd find a proper watering can soon enough, and spilled water wasn't top of mind anyway.

The metal first ad kit was rusty but the contents clean. He unspooled a long length of bandage and tore off strips of medical tape to be ready. Unwrapping the splints from his broken fingers, Leech pressed his hand flat against the cold floor, hissing from the pain. He didn't think it would matter if he used one of the already broken fingers—and pinkies being all the rage, he placed the sharp end of a fat butcher's knife against the point of the break.

Sondheim's *Pacific Overtures* reached a crescendo and he leaned on the blade with his weight, crying out as the steel severed the last digit of his pinky with a wet pop.

He rocked back on his knees and dropped the knife, panting as he clutched the wounded hand to his chest, and had to blink tears from his eyes as he wrapped the waiting bandage around the oozing finger.

The severed bit of him sat on the floor in a gleaming puddle of dark red and he snatched it up, shuffling on his knees until he could jam the finger down into the dirt alongside the thick stem of the marijuana plant. He planned to conceal the pot in the cupboard with a grow light, but wasn't sure if he should remove the marijuana. Maybe the growing vegetable god would want to consume it. Heck, might even decide that taking on the form of a marijuana plant was the optimal path for survival.

But he didn't think so. He thought Yggrdrasil would soon be towering overhead in all its mushroom glory. He would take it down into the basement where it could flourish and grow strong in the dark.

In return, he would ask it to keep the Hungry Devil trapped in the well.

Rising on shaky legs, Leech relit his fallen joint and made his way to Don's wall of homemade records.

The record that got Don killed was titled *Doomsday* and the track listing was filled out by hand. Ten tracks, most of them foreign names. World leader types Leech recognized from the news. The first was different and simply read EUROPEAN UNION BANKING. He thought about what the devil would let Don record and didn't think any of the guys back at Control would have recognized his smile.

Leech lit another joint and put the gleaming metal record on turntable number two. His vision shimmered as he played with the power knobs on the console, turned everything up to ten. The fillings in his back teeth buzzed and static electricity lifted the short hairs on his forearms. He thought the signal would reach Europe easily. Canada for sure. The main body of the United States. Further.

The devil laughed.

Leech grabbed the boom mic and leaned in. "To the folks at home and all the ships at sea, it's Archie Leech coming at you from the top of the world. I want to play something special, a last gasp from DJ Don." He pushed off the console and the chair rolled over to the turntables. Lifting the needle into place, Leech rolled back to the mic. "This one's dedicated to the real happening crew who think they're in Control."

The ground vibrated beneath his feet and he could hear the shriek of tortured metal outside as great concave dishes rotated. The devil reached out across the miles as the pop and hiss of a bad recording filled the air. Leech pressed hands over his ears. God it was loud. Shouting in French. Whatever the guy was saying would surely upset somebody.

He grinned, tasting blood when his nose sprang a leak. "Fuck you."

The phone rang and Leech wiped blood on his pants

before turning down the in-studio volume. A blue spark jumped from his finger to the control panel. The place was thrumming with a static charge.

Leech answered the phone. "KZXX request line."

"Oh baby!" Karen said and it went the way Don said it would. Karen's voice filled the studio and Leech pushed back in the chair, holding his Zippo to the joint. His heart and the joint smoldered in tandem while she cried and Control threatened.

Karen sounded scared enough that Leech almost blew his play. Almost decided to bring the whole house of cards down on their heads so he could hear them scream.

Instead he waited for the voice from Control to pause for breath and said, "Shut up and check the European stock market."

"What?"

"Do it, asshole."

He heard muffled voices and then the speaker returned. "What have you done?"

"Even if you have a missile in the air right this minute, I can broadcast enough to crash the world economy. To shove America the beautiful right into war."

"Now listen—"

"Don't ever interrupt me."

The speaker went quiet. He was still there, his breathing audible, but he was waiting. If Leech needed confirmation about the size of the weapon he was sitting on, that was it.

"I have killed the DJ and sated the Hungry Devil," Leech said. "I have planted Yggrdrasil in the darkness where it will flourish and grow strong. White Bear facility is offline. You have lost your White Bear privileges. You come up, I broadcast and the tanks roll in Europe. You send those Inuit women against me and I broadcast, your economy crashes and people starve. You harm Karen and I will crack this world in two, do you understand?"

Breathing. Harsh. "What do you want?"

"You bring Karen up here within seventy-two hours, unharmed. If she's not here, I broadcast. If she's been harmed, I broadcast. I make you this promise . . . no one will ever use White Bear station against you if you abide by our deal. Yggdrasil will protect White Bear station. I'll keep playing records to keep the Hungry Devil mollified in his well."

The response was quick. "Deal."

Leech followed the instructions Don left for him and reoriented the dishes to listen in on Control. He wanted to memorialize their conversation in case someone's memory developed a hitch.

Don's record press looked complex but wasn't hard to operate once Leech played around with it. The notes said something about magnetic fields from the special recordings wiping tapes after only a few minutes. Had to lay those tracks down on an album if he wanted the recording to last.

Leech used the press the way Don instructed, fed in a blank steel disc and listened to the scritch-scratch as Control's chatter was transferred. In another life he would have thought it was pretty cool.

Disconnecting, he cried a little bit, smoked a bit of weed and hoped Karen was comforted by the thought of seeing him again, even if she didn't like the cold. He hoped the Control operatives were nice to her.

Leech walked towards the door, careful in the manner of an old man. He stepped out into the cacophony of a hundred speakers in the trees. Snowflakes danced like agitated electrons and pine boughs shed their white mantles with the muffled *whumpf* of distant explosions.

The wind plucked the joint from his mouth and Leech held onto the doorframe. He hoped he wouldn't get shot before he reached some accommodation with the Inuit women.

If Karen didn't arrive alive and whole, he was resolved to put the *Doomsday* album back on the turntable. He'd skip over the initial recordings right to the last one.

Track ten: "The President of the United States."

The human world would burn and Yggdrasil would rise from the ashes.

He was Archibald Leech, with a devil in the well and a demigod in the cupboard. The end of his story had yet to be written.

ACKNOWLEDGMENTS

No book is written alone. Well, technically it is written alone but it's written with a tremendous amount of support from people and occasionally dogs. First I have to thank Max Booth III and Lori Michelle for gritting their teeth to go another round with me and make a book. I also have to thank my writing group Who Wants Cake, for enjoying Archibald Leech enough that I was encouraged to write another story about him and then another until I realized, holy shit, this is a book. I need to thank a great writer and even better human being John F.D. Taff for checking in with me several times during these strange years of lockdown and isolation. As always, Coraline, my ever enthusiastic pitbull-shepherd mix reminds me to lighten up and get a snack . . . but seriously, she is a steady reminder of what's really important in this world. And last but not least, my wife Linda Jones, who not only reads the first, terrible draft of everything I write, but lets me barge into her office to read whatever bit I've just written and listens as I describe intricacies of plot and story that are clear in my mind but must sound like a madman's ravings to anyone not actually inside my head.

ABOUT THE AUTHOR

John C. Foster was born in Sleepy Hollow, New York, and has been afraid of the dark for as long as he can remember. He is the author of the crime thriller *Rooster* and four previous novels, *The Isle*, *Dead Men*, *Night Roads* and *Mister White*, as well as one collection of short stories, *Baby Powder and Other Terrifying Substances*. His stories have appeared in magazines and anthologies including *Dark Moon Digest*, *Strange Aeons*, *Dark Visions Volume 2* and *Lost Films*, among others. He lives in Brooklyn with the actress Linda Jones and their dog Coraline. For more information, please visit www.johnfosterfiction.com.

SPOOKY TALES FROM GHOULISH BOOKS

☐**BELOW | Laurel Hightower**
ISBN: 978-1-943720-69-9 $12.95
A creature feature about a recently divorced woman trying to survive a road trip through the mountains of West Virginia.

☐**MAGGOTS SCREAMING! | Max Booth III**
ISBN: 978-1-943720-68-2 $18.95
On a hot summer weekend in San Antonio, Texas, a father and son bond after discovering three impossible corpses buried in their back yard.

☐**LEECH | John C. Foster**
ISBN: 978-1-943720-70-5 $14.95
Horror / noir mashup about a top secret government agency's most dangerous employee. Doppelgangers, demigods, and revenants, oh my!

☐**ALL THESE SUBTLE DECEITS | C.S. Humble**
ISBN: 978-1-943720-71-2 $14.95
A possessed woman and an exorcist descend into an occult labyrinth of dark forces and oppressive spirits.

☐**RABBITS IN THE GARDEN | Jessica McHugh**
ISBN: 978-1-943720-73-6 $16.95
13-year-old Avery Norton is a crazed killer—according to the staff at Taunton Asylum, anyway. But as she struggles to prove her innocence in the aftermath of gruesome murders spanning the 1950s, Avery discovers there's a darker force keeping her locked away . . . which she calls "Mom."

☐**PERFECT UNION | Cody Goodfellow**
ISBN: 978-1-943720-74-3 $18.95
Three brothers searching the wilderness for their mother instead find a utopian cult that seeks to reinvent society, family . . . humanity

Patreon:
www.patreon.com/pmmpublishing

Website:
www.PerpetualPublishing.com

Facebook:
www.facebook.com/PerpetualPublishing

Twitter:
@PMMPublishing

Newsletter:
www.PMMPNews.com

Email Us:
Contact@PerpetualPublishing.com

CPSIA information can be obtained
at www.ICGtesting.com
Printed in the USA
LVHW031349040822
725043LV00002B/127